Advance praise for *The Shadow*

"There are certain books I pull down from my shelves to remind me of the magic and the mystery of the real Mexico, the Mexico of the *campo*. Among my favorites are Juan Rulfo's *Pedro Paramo*, Graham Greene's *The Power and the Glory*, and Harriet Doerr's *Stones for Ibarra*. Now I have a new favorite: Américo Paredes's *The Shadow*. Through his rich language, Paredes has etched in this slim, powerful work characters who will haunt my memory."

—Patrick Oster,
author of *The Mexicans: A Personal Portrait of a People*

Praise for Américo Paredes

"A voice that is direct, intimate, and colloquial, engaging the reader immediately."

—*Publishers Weekly*

"Paredes' forays into literature . . . are fierce, inventive, and prescient in their approach to the pressing concerns of their— and our—times."

—Jane Creighton, *Houston Chronicle*

"A talented and admirable Southwestern writer."

—James Sanderson, *Texas Books in Review*

(please turn the page for more rave reviews)

Praise for Américo Paredes's previous novel, *George Washington Gómez*

"At once deeply sympathetic, even optimistic, and powerfully satirical . . . Narrated with such deep humanity that differences of era, culture, and race are over-ridden . . . Paredes evokes boyhood with more sympathy than anyone since Dickens."

—John Herndon, *Austin American-Statesman*

"An absorbing, heart-rending story told with sensitivity and wisdom . . . The content and style of the novel transcend racial or national divisions . . . A lively narrative . . . Readers will find much to admire in this fine novel."

—*Beaumont Enterprise*

Praise for Américo Paredes's collected short fiction, *The Hammon and the Beans*

Praise for Américo Paredes's humorous folklore collection, *Uncle Remus con chile*

"Renowned folklorist Paredes has gather intracultural stories which suggest the range of attitude, including conflict, that Mexicans and Mexican Texans have toward Anglo America . . . All-inclusive in mood and tone, the stories demonstrate all types of humor, including at times a biting wit."
—*Books of the Southwest*

Praise for Américo Paredes's selected poems, *Between Two Worlds*

"A long-overdue collection . . . This volume may be considered a forerunner to the flourishing of Chicano literature that has taken place in the last few decades . . . The poems selected for inclusion in this book are worth reading not only for their literary value, but for their historical value as well."
—*Review of Texas Books*

The Shadow

Books by Américo Paredes

Fiction

George Washington Gómez: A Mexicotexan Novel

The Hammon and the Beans and Other Stories

The Shadow

Non-Fiction

Folklore and Culture on the Texas-Mexican Border

Folktales of Mexico

A Texas-Mexican Cancionero:
Folksongs of the Lower Border

Uncle Remus con chile

With His Pistol in His Hand: A Border Ballad and Its Hero

Poetry

Cantos de Adolescencia
Between Two Worlds

Co-Author

Folk Music of Mexico
(with Joseph Castle)

Mexican-American Authors
(with Raymund Paredes)

Toward New Perspectives in Folklore
(with Richard Bauman)

The Urban Experience and Folk Tradition
(with Ellen Stekert)

The Shadow

Américo Paredes

Arte Público Press
Houston, Texas
1998

This volume is made possible through grants from the National Endowment for the Arts (a federal agency), Andrew W. Mellon Foundation, and the City of Houston through The Cultural Arts Council of Houston, Harris County.

Recovering the past, creating the future

Arte Público Press
University of Houston
Houston, Texas 77204-2090

Cover illustration and design by Giovanni Mora

Paredes, Américo.
   The Shadow / by Américo Paredes.
   p.   cm.
   ISBN 1-55885-230-1 (alk. paper)
   1. Mexico — History — Revolution, 1910-1920 — Veterans — Fiction. I. Title.
PS3531.A525S54   1998
813'.54—dc21
                                     98-10313
                                        CIP

∞ The paper used in this publication meets the requirements of the American National Standard for Information Sciences—Permanence of Paper for Printed Library Materials, ANSI Z39.48-1984.

8 9 0 1 2 3 4 5 6 7   10 9 8 7 6 5 4 3 2 1

Preface

In the 1950s, I decided to enter a novel-writing contest. Not that I didn't have anything else to do. I was taking graduate courses in English and Spanish, teaching a couple of freshman English courses, and doing research for my dissertation. But first prize in the contest was $500, an impressive sum for a graduate student with a wife and two children.

I won, with a novel called *The Shadow*. It was a welcome boost to the family bank account and to my ego as well. Everybody liked my novel: friends, teachers, colleagues. And the contest judges, of course.

Everybody, that is, except editors and publishers. Within a few months, *The Shadow had* garnered a goodly number of rejection slips. Not as many as a short story of mine called "The Hammon and the Beans," but then that story had been making the rounds since 1939.

Friends thought that a few additions and revisions would make the novel publishable. They made suggestions—many suggestions. Some of them looked good to me, so I added them to the manuscript, patching and mending here and there. Still no takers. Finally I gave up and turned to projects that held more promise, such as finishing my dissertation.

Only very recently have I come back to *The Shadow* and attempted to restore it to its original form. It has been a job more of excision than of revision. I may have cut too close to the bone, because this version seems shorter than the original. Again, it may be that forty years ago the original had

Preface

seemed longer than it was. "The Hammon and the Beans," by the way, did make it into print some years ago, and it has been doing well.

Endeavors of this sort most often are sustained by the goodwill of others. So has it been for me in the past, and so it is now. I am particularly indebted to three good friends: To Pat Jasper and Tara Holley for keeping me from becoming mobility impaired these many months. And to Frances Terry, as always, for her patience and expertise in the preparation of the manuscript.

Muchísimas gracias.

Américo Paredes

Chapter 1

The noon was a glaring quietness. There was no breeze, no movement. People were indoors, waiting for the fury of the sun to pass; outside, dogs and chickens panted in the shade-speckled dust. In the chaparral, life was also still. It had sought the cool, dark places and lay hidden from sight. There was a heavy loneliness in the hour, as if the whole world were dead.

Only at the communal farm of Los Claveles was anyone astir. There, men in sandals and white cotton drawers worked in the fields, plowing the rapidly drying earth. They worked against time—time lost earlier in the year while their leaders made trips to nearby Morelos to talk to the authorities, while they sent petitions to Mexico City, while they marched through the old settlements where lived the original owners of the land they had "affected" and turned into an agrarian colony. Now they had the land, and they were working it, though they would have preferred to be in the shade like all men with some sense in their heads. But they stayed in the fields because Antonio Cuitla, president of the *ejido*, kept them there.

That noon Cuitla was riding down a lonely wagon trail, the fields on his left, the unfenced chaparral on his right. His eyes were on the fields. Calm, thoughtful eyes, wrinkled at the corners from too much squinting into the distance. Too soft for the stern angularity of his face, except when he screwed them almost shut to look across the quaking, heat-shimmered distance at his men working in the fields.

Américo Paredes

He was a man in his forties, with that hewn appearance of limb and features sometimes found in mestizos who have much Indian ancestry, and he sat his horse easily, almost proudly. The sorrel plodded along on top of its own shadow, its hoofs plumping noiselessly into the fine alkali dust, which rose in a mist about horse and rider. It coated the shiny metal of the .30-30 rifle across his saddle horn, worked into the seams of his leather-colored face and stuck there, mixed with sweat. It dulled the angry brilliance of the red-silk kerchief Cuitla had about his throat.

Except for the kerchief, Antonio Cuitla's clothes were in the American style: yellow drill trousers, heavy shapeless shoes, and a blue work shirt. Even his straw hat was shaped and blocked in the manner of a Texan felt hat. But he wore it at the back of his head, letting a lock of graying hair hang over his forehead like a cock's comb. His shirttails, gathered outside his belt and tied in a knot over his navel, were another concession to the customs of his native village.

In the distance, the men still worked, and Cuitla peered at them through the glare with half-shut eyes. He saw them and he did not, for as he looked he did not see skinny little men in cotton drawers, sun-shriveled men sweating their lives into the sun-baked land. He saw green, waving fields, networks of canals, white-washed houses, trim fences, and flower-bordered lanes. And moving about them a brown and happy race: harvesting, feasting, playing. And in the foreground, looking straight at him with confidence in his eyes, stood a brawny farmer, his child on his shoulder, his young wife by the hand, and all three smiling at him with strong, white teeth, smiles of contentment and cleanliness and health. And it was all in several colors, as he had seen it many years ago on the cover of an educational magazine.

Then the picture was gone, and he saw his men in the distance, like little white dolls against the gray-green of the chaparral. He thought of the puppets he had seen on a street-corner in Mexico City once, when he had been there with the occupying forces. He had been a young man then, a common soldier, and his captain had ordered him to take a man to the cemetery, where the firing squads were. An old man who talked to him all the way there.

Suddenly it was cold. A chill went through him, and the rifle shook in his grasp. Just slightly. He put his free hand to his face and kneaded his forehead with the palm of his hand until the coldness went away. As he took his hand from his eyes, he said to himself, "It must be done, for their own sakes, though it is never pleasant. But I'll do it for them."

He knew them well and he loved them. He had led them for a long time during the years of war, the years of killing other men who looked like you and talked like you. He remembered the old man again. He had been ordered to take him to the cemetery because he belonged to the other side. And the old man kept saying, "Aren't we all the same? Aren't we all the same?" All the way to the cemetery, and he didn't stop until the volley cut him short.

He had felt cold then, too. "They do not know," he told himself. "They are Indians without shoes, how can they know? They love the land, but they were born too soon. It is up to me to know for them, for their children's sake. That is my burden and my pride."

He liked the sound of those last words: "my burden and my pride." It always pleased him when he thought up phrases like that. He repeated the words aloud, to get the full satisfaction they could give, to feel them in his mouth like a morsel. He said them aloud, and the sound of his voice was so strange in the breathless silence that he stopped his horse in the middle of the road. When he spoke, it had seemed to him that the distance had answered him. He cleared his throat and twisted about in his saddle to hear its reassuring creaking sound. Then he laughed, a short little laugh. He must not think about it now.

He must go find Del Toro. Meanwhile he would watch the men in the fields. They were a pretty sight. Yes. Pretty was the word. Men working their own fields, raising a crop that would be theirs and not another man's, who had not ached and sweated for it. It was a pretty sight, except for that big . . .

He turned again toward the fields and found that the men had left their work and disappeared into the brush. He caught sight of the last two of them running for the shade. That was one thing they went to in a hurry, to rest. And to eat. One of them had left his mule and plow in the middle of a furrow. He must find out who he was. Who else but a man with shit for brains would leave a costly animal out in the sun?

He gave the reins an impatient shake. He must get where he was going, and do what he had to do. "He's a wrecker, a destroyer!" That was what he had told his wife the day before. "He will ruin all that I have worked for!"

His wife listened to him as she always did, standing before him as he sat in the chair before the table, her hands folded in front of her, one eye on the food cooking in the chimney. "He loves trouble," he told her. "He does not love the land."

"I think he does love the land," she replied. "Just like you."

"Don't be a fool."

"We see people's faces, but we do not know their hearts."

"Can't you speak in your own voice? Without using those stupid proverbs all the time? Besides, that saying of yours is used for a man who is a hypocrite, who hides the way he really feels."

She did not answer. He stared gloomily at the mud-chinked wall across the table, his elbows on the rough pine boards. Then he said, "I gave them the land. I could have stayed in the army, but I wanted them to get the land."

"You could have been a general by now," she said quickly.

"Well, a colonel perhaps. At least a colonel. But I got them the land. And now they act like fools."

"They are ungrateful."

"It's that bastard, stirring them up, egging them on to take over more land when they should be working what they have."

"They are ungrateful," she repeated.

"He did everything but call me a coward in front of all the men. Because I won't drive the Jiménezes from their lands. Like our comrades at La Rosita, he says. Dragged their houses out onto the road and left them there."

"You wouldn't want to do that to Don José María."

"Can't they see that politics is part of the game? The owners at La Rosita do not belong to the party, so no one will speak for them. But the Jiménezes are big in the party. We would have the army on our butts in no time. I told them so last night! I hate even to remember it!"

"I was watching. I just felt I had to go and I was in the shadows beyond the fire. He insulted you."

"Just because he was wearing his pistol. As always. If only I had taken my rifle! I would have killed him then and there!"

"Hush," she said. "You must not say things like that, not about a comrade and old friend."

"Comrade, friend. Dog!" he cried, banging his fist on the table. "There is a limit to what a man can stand!"

It had just been talk then, but he had thought about it during the night. And today it was no longer time to think about it.

It was in Tula canyon where the devil met Rivera. But no, that was not the song. He tried hard to remember it. He had put those songs away a long time ago. They were childish, a waste of time. But now he wanted to remember this particular one, so he could quote a line from it. When they came up to him after the sound of the shots. *La defensa es permitida.* That was it. A man must defend himself. That would convince them.

They talked and thought in terms of songs and tales. Like children.

"There is something childlike about the primitive mind," Don José María had said one afternoon, "something unspoiled that appeals to one's poetic side. It is a mind, in some respects, in the first stage of innocence." He was toying with his coffee cup as he sat at a table in the shade of Cuitla's hut, pretending to drink but merely bringing the cup to his lips now and then, just enough to leave a few creamy drops on the brush of his reddish-brown mustache.

"I don't know about that," Cuitla said. "Of course you are right in general, I would not dare to dispute your greater wisdom. But you don't know these people like I do."

He spoke partly from pride, and also from a desire to contribute to the conversation. For the most part he preferred to listen to Don José María, feeling that in these talks there was something literary, something cultured and elevated. Cuitla added, "Perhaps you have not seen them with their holiday clothes on, as the saying goes."

Don José María shrugged and touched the coffee cup to his lips. "Know that they are cruel?" he answered, putting the

cup down again. "But my dear sir, children are also cruel. Did
you read about the little boy who cut his baby brother's throat
just the other day? It was in the papers. Their father is a
butcher. Why, children are as cruel and as ignorant as any
barefoot Indian."

Cuitla glanced down at his shoes.

"There is something poetic about them, though," Don
José María added.

Cuitla said gently, nodding his head, "But corn is more
important."

"You are right," Don José María said. "And you well
know how much I agree with you, how much I would like to
see all these people, who are our people, yours and mine,"—
he included Cuitla in the same category as himself with a
broad wave of his hand—"well fed, well shod."

"I know your interest," Cuitla replied. "I am grateful for it
and shall always be."

They had just finished going over the agrarian code. Don
José María had been explaining some difficult passages to
Cuitla so that he could know the full extent of his rights.

"Yes," Don José María said, "the man in huaraches has
a place close to my heart. And his welfare for me too is the
first of all things. But in hailing the dawn of a new and better
day, one may also regret the charm of the sun that is setting.
You are too near them." He tapped his fingers on the table
close to Cuitla's arm. "Not that you are like them, or really
one of them. There is too much ambition, too much imagi-
nation, too much soul in such a man as you."

Cuitla looked at the ground between his legs, embarrassed.

"Temperamentally," Don José María continued, "you and
I are much closer to each other than to them. But you are too
near to them physically, so perhaps it is difficult for you to
appreciate their charm.

Américo Paredes

"It engages one's heart, even though," he smiled ruefully, "even though that childlike impulsiveness may result in the grief of the admirer. The thorn in the rose," he said, putting down the coffee cup again and imitating the opening of a flower with his hands.

"You can put your mind at ease," Cuitla said. "I can assure you that the matter will not go any further than it has already gone."

"I have faith in you," Don José María answered. "You are a reasonable man."

"Too many false stories have been told about us. We are not bandits, we are not robbers. We only want a little corner of the earth, which belongs to all of us."

"Rightly so, rightly so. And have any of us here, the old own—the old inhabitants of the section, really opposed it? Well, some of the less wise, the less far-seeing, perhaps, but not I. It was not the government that forced me to part with those pastures that you got from me, nor any show of force. That was my contribution, and I would willingly have given it—more even. If it had been needed, of course."

"I know your heart," Cuitla said gently. "It is not like many of the others. But even the others, and more so you, have rights also. I see that, and I have explained it to them more than once. We have land, you have land. Why should we not be neighbors and live in peace?"

"Such is my wish, with all my heart."

"So it shall be."

"I wish you luck. They are good men, very good men, but some foolish ideas have been put into their heads."

"They will listen to me," Cuitla said firmly. "It is I who have made them what they are. Who has led them? Coaxed them? Kept them going when they would rather have thrown down their rifles and gone home? And keep them working

8

now, when they would like to sit in the shade and drink themselves stupid?"

"You can feel proud, quite proud of what you have done."

"But they are so stupidly stubborn sometimes."

"Why, it is the child in them again," Don José María said,
again raising the ever-full coffee cup to his lips. "You offered
them the sugar-plum of the future, and they listened to everything you said. Now the future is here, but it does not taste so
sweet; there is sweat mingled with it."

This was so close to Cuitla's own thoughts that he forgot
himself and cried out angrily, "Oh God, God, God!" And he
banged on the table so hard that he startled Don José María
into taking a full swallow of coffee, on which he choked and
sputtered until he spit most of it out upon the ground.

Sometimes he felt he could kill them all with his bare
hands. But to punish them was like cutting away part of himself. Once, when he was a boy, a thorn had gotten into his
heel, deep below the protecting callus, and built itself a little
chamber of yellow pus. He took a knife and cut into the callus, and below it, reaching down to the thorn, while the pain
turned his mouth into a saltish slobber. Then joy and relief
when he finally got the thorn out and squeezed until red,
healthy blood came forth.

A man must defend himself. He would wound himself
with Del Toro's revolver, just slightly, before the others came.

His eyes, focused inwardly, came slowly and reluctantly
to the actual world, to Antonio Cuitla riding along the dusty
trail. And it was then that he saw it.

He saw it for an instant out of the corner of his eye. He
jerked his head toward it, as the horse stopped short. The
sorrel shrank back, back and down, as though gathering itself
for one tremendous leap.

Américo Paredes

The shadow was just beyond the animal's head. It was a dense, shapeless mass of black rising out of the middle of the road, where no shadow should be. It made no movement or sound. It was just there in the bright silence of noon.

The horse shied, shaking its head. Then the shadow was gone. There was nothing on the dust of the road but the reflected brilliance of the sun.

He slid off the trembling horse. For a moment he stood beside it, breathing heavily, one hand clutching the pommel, the other holding his rifle. When his legs felt stronger, he went forward and examined the ground.

There were no tracks in the soft dirt. He looked at the trees and the underbrush by the side of the road. Nothing. The chaparral was still with the lonely stillness of noon.

There was nothing there.

Chapter 2

Nothing at all. Fool! Frightened by nothing, like a super-
stitious Indian. A man like him, who had read books and
seen other countries. It was not for him to go around seeing
shadows on the road. He thought with shame that he had
almost fired his gun. That would have ruined everything.

But it was over now. He was jumpy, that was all.

Still, he squatted in the middle of the road, one hand holding the reins, the rifle butt braced against the ground with the
other, peering at the spot where he had seen—where he had
thought he had seen—the thing. All he saw now was the fine,
powdery dust of the road. Undisturbed. Slowly he rose to his
feet, his joints aching. The trembling in his legs enraged him,
and he cursed them as if they belonged to someone else. It
made him feel better, and his legs grew stronger.

His step grew firmer as he led the horse to the shade of
a large ebony that grew beside the road. He sat down against
the trunk with a sigh that was tremulous in spite of himself.
The horse tugged at the reins, and he stretched out his arm
to give the animal room to raise its head. He would sit here
for a few moments. Before he moved on, he must be com-
pletely calm.

He shut his eyes and tried to marshal in his mind the
arguments he would have used if another man had come up
to him with the story that he had been frightened by a ghost,
a shadow on the road, in the middle of the day.

He tried to concentrate, but the horse kept pulling at the
reins and jerking his arm. It kept raising its head and looking

into the underbrush beyond the tree. Now and then it would point its ears forward, like two hairy fingers, and look steadily into the chaparral. Then it would lower its head, only to raise it again.

Cuitla peered into the underbrush, suppressing a chill that twitched at his back: the thought that the horse saw something he could not see, something that had shown itself around a corner of his mind, for just an instant. But he had better sense than that.

It must have been a dizzy spell. He had not been feeling well lately. Perhaps he had a cold. For the past couple of days he had been thinking of sending to Morelos for some medicine. A few times he had seen spots before his eyes, and what was this shadow but a big spot? A great black spot in the middle of the road. That would have given him a blackness before his eyes, inside his eyes really. The spot, the shadow, the black shapeless mass. It had been inside his head. Not in the middle of the road.

But the horse had shied. It had stopped in its tracks and shied, so suddenly that Cuitla almost lost his seat. It had started sideways when he saw the black thing. Surely the horse . . .

It was hard to explain *that* with dizzy spells and spots before his eyes. Yes, there was the horse. The heavy coldness that had begun to lift from Cuitla's stomach bore down on him again.

Then the horse lifted its head once more, jerking sharply at his arm. Cuitla looked up at the animal. He had jerked at the reins, that was it!

He tried to remember if he had pulled the reins just before the horse stopped, in that instant between The shadow's appearance and the shying of the horse. After a moment's effort he became convinced that he had done so. He had pulled at the reins.

He must have started back in his saddle and jerked at the reins. The curb bit had done the rest. He smiled. It was a good thing he was a man who could reason things out. A thinking, reasonable man.

Another man wouldn't have thought the matter out, and he would have given superstition one more point to stand on, with his story about seeing a shadow in the middle of the road at noon. It was worse if the man happened to be known as truthful and honest. Superstition was strengthened, and it became harder to combat the darkness in the minds of the people. Some day all men would be reasonable, and such things would not be. But, meanwhile, Antonio Cuitla was greatly relieved that he, at least, was a reasoning man and had thought the matter out.

Now he must get going, down to the south corner field. It was just a little plot, screened on three sides by chaparral, and on this plot Del Toro was plowing, all by himself, since he had claimed this bit of rich soil as his own. Probably under a tree now, eating his noonday meal. After it was all over, Cuitla would shoot himself, just a graze, with Del Toro's revolver.

He rose, pulling at the reins to bring the horse closer to him, but the horse resisted. It was still looking into the under-brush. Cuitla went up to it and put his hand on the saddle. The horse kept looking into the brush. Again it pointed its ears forward.

Cuitla looked also, and saw the brush move a few yards away. It was a very slight movement, as though a faint wind had stirred the branches, but there was no wind. He waited, scarcely breathing, his eyes fixed on the brush. The horse was looking too, its ears still pointed forward.

Américo Paredes

The top of a branch whipped upward and danced wildly for a moment. Then its oscillations lessened until its movement became a gentle rocking that gradually vanished.

Cuitla leaped away from the horse and put his back against the ebony, flattening himself against the trunk. The branches moved again, a little faster now.

"Out of there!" Cuitla cried.

The movement stopped. Then it began again, much slower now, inching toward him, but boldly almost, as if the thing moving toward him through the brush preferred to let him know it was coming, though it did not yet choose to show itself.

A sudden, bristling terror seized him. He raised his rifle and fired at the moving branches. Again and again he fired, without aiming, until the movement ceased. Then he waited, his breath coming in quick gasps. The thing did not move again. Still Cuitla waited, leaning back against the bole of the ebony, fighting an overwhelming desire to slide down against it and sit on its roots. Little by little his head cleared. He looked down at his rifle and slipped a few more cartridges into the magazine.

Then, with a cursing resolve, he picked his way forward, moving toward the spot into which he had fired. He pushed away the branches with one hand and held the rifle in the other, ready to fire, ready to strike out with the butt, ready to fight with his fingernails if he had to. He told himself that he would do just that, stand his ground and fight it, whatever it was.

And among the broken branches he found a man. A city man, dressed in a striped silk shirt and black trousers. One of his shiny, lowcut shoes was soiled with fresh manure. A new felt hat lay close to the body, and a fine automatic pistol was lying near the right hand. The body did not have much of a head. One of Cuitla's soft-nosed bullets had burst it open.

Just a man. A puny little city man, scarcely more than a boy. A skinny little boy from the city, who had come looking for trouble among real men and found more than he had bargained for. Cuitla felt like throwing back his head and laughing. He patted his rifle. Old ghost killer, his little .30-30. For a moment there he had almost . . .

But he hadn't really. He had known it was a man all along. Wait till he told the men tonight, how the fellow had tried to ambush him. Tonight. He had forgotten. There would be a meeting tonight, and Del Toro would be there.

"Meddler!" he hissed at the dead man. "Meddling son-of-a-bitch!" He spat on the bloody remnant of a head.

Even now, he knew, the men of the colony were running across the fields toward the sound of the shots, Del Toro at their head. Shouting orders, the bastard. Del Toro would come to his rescue.

But they did not come. Cuitla waited for some moments beside the body and then went out to the road again, thinking about the meeting that night. Gloomily, he came out to the edge of the brush and saw them, far across the fields. They were coming, but very slowly and strung out in a line.

He expelled his breath in an exasperated "Agh!" Was there anything they could do right if he was not there to tell them how? He stepped across the road to the edge of the fields and yelled at them. They stopped, and he yelled again and waved. They remained where they were, looking across the fields at him. He swung his rifle in a movement that meant "come" and they broke into a trot, still in a wavering, strung-out line.

Cuitla went back across the road, leaned against the trunk of the ebony, and watched them come. When they got nearer, they stopped trotting and walked the rest of the way, drawing their line a little tighter, their rifles at ready. Dark little men, little men who walked in shuffling steps, little men dressed in thin white drawers and tunics, their feet in sandals made of pieces of rawhide and old tire casings. These were his men.

Now they were close enough so he could see their faces. Warily they came up until they were within a few paces from him. They stopped then and formed a semicircle around him, their weapons still poised, looking at him in silence, waiting for him to tell them what to do. Cuitla just stared at them, still leaning against the ebony.

Old Juan Sánchez stepped out of the semicircle and came closer to Cuitla, looking into his face with his veiled, crafty eyes.

"It *is* him," Juan Sánchez said.

Cuitla gave him a look of bored patience. Then he snorted and looked away.

"Did those shots come from here, *jefe?*" Sánchez asked.

"From where else, you old fool?" Cuitla told him.

"That's what we thought," Sánchez said. "But we weren't sure—you know how those things are. It's pretty hard to locate the direction of a shot in the woods, as you well know. As I was saying to Serapio just a moment ago, he was too young during the Revolution, but you remember the time—"

"Keep your stories for another day," Cuitla said sharply.

"As you say, *jefe,*" Sánchez replied, "but as I was saying, we heard the shots and—"

"And you and these other fools decided to promenade over here by and by," Cuitla broke in. "Where did you think you were? At the plaza?"

Sánchez's face assumed a look of tolerant repentance. The others were embarrassed and looked down at their toes.

"One would think you were born yesterday," Cuitla went on. "One would think you had never been under fire in all your lives."

Even Sánchez looked embarrassed now. They all stared at the ground, still in a semicircle before him. Cuitla let them stay like that for a few moments. Then he flicked away a twig with which he had been picking his teeth and moved slowly toward his horse. The men parted respectfully to let him pass. He reached the horse and put his hand on the bridle. Not until then did he turn and jerk his head toward the brush.

"There's a dead man in there," he announced.

"The outsider?" Sánchez asked.

Cuitla stopped, his hand on the saddle horn.

"We were following him," Sánchez explained. "As I was telling you, we were following him and just didn't know which way he had taken, but we were following his tracks. Pretty foolish, the way he went through the brush, though what can you expect of a man who wears pointed shoes. But we were after him, and that's why we came so slow after we heard your shots. We just didn't know, and after what had just happened we had to be careful. He killed Del Toro just a tiny little while ago."

Cuitla clutched at the saddle horn to steady himself. When he turned toward Sánchez, the old man was staring at him. Cuitla stared back, and Sánchez dropped his eyes.

"Well," Cuitla said. "You'll find him in the brush, a little ways in there."

"He must have wanted to get you both," another of the men said. "The sly son-of-a-bitch. And we thought he didn't know where he was going, the way his trail zigzagged."

"Perhaps," Cuitla said, looking thoughtfully toward the brush.

When he looked back, he again met Sánchez's shrewd eyes, small and cunning, fleshy under the white eyebrows.

"That rag the *presidente* is wearing around his neck," Sánchez said. "It must have made a fine target. There's nothing that stands out better in the woods than a red cloth."

Américo Paredes

Cuitla frowned. Why had he worn the damn thing anyway? He, for whom the ultimate symbol of frivolity was the silver-decorated peon's hat. Gaudiness, effeminacy, ease—those things he had put away from himself long ago. And now this red rag.

He had bought it for his wife. On one of his trips to Morelos he had bought the red kerchief for her, so she could wear it about her neck in the way she had worn other red kerchiefs in her young days, when she was a soldier's woman, his woman, following him all the way up to the battle line to bring him his tortillas and to pass him cartridges while he fought. He could not explain now the sudden impulse, the abrupt bravado that had made him, just as he left the house to look for Del Toro, take the kerchief down from its nail by the door and knot it around his neck, a brave bit of color burning bright against his sober clothes. So he made a joke of it.

"Yes," he laughed, touching the red cloth with his fingertips. "I wanted to give him a good target. I wanted to give him some odds."

The men chuckled. "Ah!" they said. "All heart and *cojones*, that's our *presidente*."

"Where were you when you wove into him, chief?" asked one of them.

"About two or three paces from the ebony."

"And he was in the brush?"

"God, that was a bad spot!"

"Your guardian angel must have been hovering over you."

Cuitla slapped the stock of his rifle. "*This* is my guardian angel. Sánchez!" he shouted. "I want you to take charge of the bodies."

Sánchez touched his straw hat briefly and was silent, looking at Cuitla with his shrewd, steady stare.

"Have some men take Del Toro home. Then have a detail bury the other one."

Sánchez touched his hat again. Then he turned to the others. "Anastacio," he said softly. "Take five men with you and go carry the late Del Toro home as the *presidente* has ordered. Get axes from the shed near the south end and cut some long saplings so you can make a litter."

Anastacio pointed at the five men nearest him, and all six left immediately at a trot, obviously glad to get away. Sánchez turned to some others, detailing them as a burial party for the stranger. His soft voice was even softer now, relaying Cuitla's shouted orders. Cuitla watched him, frowning. He's doing it on purpose, he thought, the old son-of-a-bitch.

Some of the men chosen to bury the outsider were crossing themselves before going into the brush.

"You there!" Cuitla shouted at one who had lagged behind to cross himself a second time. "Do you want a priest to go with you?"

The man grinned at the ground in the vicinity of his left foot.

"Go where you are told!" Cuitla said.

The man went.

Chapter 3

When Captain Diego Garza de Jiménez came downriver from Mier and founded the settlement that was later to be the city of Morelos, he also founded a ranch still farther downriver, and he named this ranch El Carmen de los Jiménez, The Villa of the Jiménezes. To his descendants it became simply El Carmen, and as the Jiménez family continued to grow, the vast original holdings of the captain were divided into smaller ranches, called by other names. Those who remained on the central holdings at El Carmen were distinguished from their relatives by the title of Los Jiménez del Carmen. Thus the old ranch ceased to belong to the descendants of the old Asturian captain who had founded it, and the descendants came to belong to the ranch.

When it was not necessary to distinguish one branch of the family from another, the ranch was referred to simply as El Carmen, without the appendage of the family name either before or after it. Thus was it known to its present owner, Don José María Jiménez, at least on most occasions. Only in the privacy of his parlor, when he talked to his sons about the past, did he call the ranch by its full name—El Carmen de los Jiménez—to impress upon them the glories that were lost, the grandeur that was slipping away as more and more outsiders, rank foreigners from the north and south, came into the country and slowly pushed their betters from the land.

Don José María Jiménez was a man approaching middle age, slight, straight, and supple like a quirt. His blue eyes, ruddy skin and reddish-brown mustache all betrayed the northern blood of his Spanish forebears, a blood that had been preserved like an heirloom by generations of inbreeding, of cousins marrying cousins within the area of the Jiménez holdings, so that the whole tribe had less than a half-dozen names in its family tree as far back as it could be traced. Don José María walked with a proud step, especially when he went across the river to visit Jonesville-on-the-Grande, which he still referred to by its original name of Tres Ríos.

In Jonesville-on-the-Grande he was often mistaken for an Anglo by people who did not know him, and in restaurants and other public places he was likely to be spoken to in English, a language he preferred not to understand. This always gave him a little stir of pride, but only because he could answer in Spanish, "I don't know what you are saying, sir. I do not use that sort of speech at all."

And if given a chance he would add his characteristic remark, "No, I do not speak it and never expect to do so. It is too ugly a tongue. It is a dog's tongue, like the sound of two dogs fighting. I have no need of it, why should I learn it? If Americans want to do business with me, let them learn Spanish."

He loved to walk up and down the streets of Jonesville, just to look at the new buildings, the shiny automobiles and the people always hurrying somewhere. And he would remember that much of that land was his by right, if the Americans had not come and stolen it. For the Americans had been the first outsiders to come, hungry for land, the land of the Jiménez clan, which once had straddled the river in its pride. Time had moved on and left them weak, poor and weak. They who had once been so strong and had held in their hands the lives of women and of men.

To his children, still in their teens, he loved to tell about his great-aunt María Dolores, who had died in his own house not many years before. The aunt had fallen in love with a Spanish sailor in the days when steam vessels tied at the dock of El Carmen de los Jiménez to load hides and tallow, thirty years before Don José María himself was born. The family had frowned on this unwise love for a man not born on the riverbanks, but the girl had been obstinate. The night the steamer was to sail, she made a bundle of her dearest possessions, and that night the sailor disappeared. A search was made for him, a thorough search conducted by the local authorities, all of whom were named Jiménez. The sailor was never found, and Doña María Dolores died an old maid in her great-nephew's house, which had been in happier days the house of her own father.

Those had been the great days, Don José María told his sons, when life had contained vigor and romance. But they had gone away, those times. And he would hum a stanza of the old song.

> The days that pass away
> With never any gain,
> The days that once were gay
> Have left us only pain,
> The days that have departed
> Never to come again.

And he would look away to hide the moisture in his eyes.

Even the river, which in the time of Great-Aunt Dolores had flowed before the ranch house, had gone away, as if rejecting a spot that history had passed by. It had cut a new channel and now flowed, much diminished, several miles away, and before the house was now an *estero*, a lake made by the old river bed. This lake too might soon disappear, if they had their way. There was talk of draining it and planting crops on the rich black land of its bed, for the land which had been plentiful for generations was now becoming scarce.

Don José María was against it, but he knew he was not as strong as they, and in his heart he knew that he had already lost. All he could do was long for the days when his family had been strong and united against all outside forces. In those days such tramps would have been easily dealt with. But now he and his own were going down before a wave of pajama-clad men hungry for land that was not their own, greedy for what was not theirs by right, what they had not worked for, what had not come down to them sanctified with the fragrance of past generations, past memories and past glories.

Not that Don José María was one who brooded over the past. He was known as a modern, forward-looking man. The old house that had been his forefathers'—adobe-walled and thatched with *zacahuiste* grass, and supported by enormous beams that had come from ancient ships wrecked near the rivermouth in other times—the old house still stood, with its floors of crumbling brick and its iron-barred windows, its patio in the rear, where grew dusty pomegranates and the sickly sweet oleander bloomed, and beyond that the *huisache* grove under which the beehives had buzzed until one by one they had succumbed to the poison sprayed over the cotton plants in the nearby fields. But the old house was a store-house now, where cotton was kept out of the rain and ripe corn ears were neatly stacked in bins. Saddles hung from the rafters and on the brick floors hired men spread their bedding.

José María's family lived in a modern, neat little frame house closer to the *estero's* edge, a little house with pine floors, painted white with a red roof and green shutters. Only the kitchen behind was in the old style, adobe with an adobe chimney and thatched with grass. José María had been among the first to plant cotton in a large way, and he was also, as were many of the Jiménezes, a cotton broker, who lent money on future crops to the less fortunate.

It was in the parlor of this house that José María Jiménez, heir and descendant of the founder of El Carmen de los Jiménez, sat one evening just before sunset, when the man for whom he had hoped finally appeared.

Don José María was sitting by a window, reading in the fading light. In this also did José María Jiménez show his proud descent; he was a reading and a writing man. There were books in his parlor: a copy of the novel *El Zarco*; a book on scientific agriculture; the inevitable *Bertoldo, Bertoldino y Cacaseno*; a collection of Plaza's works; and a fat notebook with manuscript copies of the verses written by his poetic great-grandfather—the old Don José María for whom he had been named. They were well-turned, witty verses, all in *décimas*, the ten-line stanza that had been popular in the Spanish court during the Golden Age. Don José María was sitting by the window looking at them, though he knew them all by heart, leafing through them, chuckling again, as he had done so many times, at the witty way in which his great-grandfather had put in his place that outsider who asked for the hand of his great-aunt María del Jesús, younger sister of the Dolores loved by the unfortunate Spanish sailor. The outsider had been a cultured man and had written well in *décimas*, too. But the old Don José María had got the better of him and sent him about his business in well-constructed and well-rhymed octosyllables.

It ran in the family, this verse-making business. The present Don José María had often tried his hand at the same thing, and now he turned to the back of the notebook—the real reason for his leafing through the collection in the first place—to look at some of his own compositions, placed fittingly at the last, after those of the old Don José María and other verse-writing Jiménezes. They were mostly satirical verses.

Of his own compositions, the young José María especially liked several bitingly comic stanzas that he had composed about the tatterdemalions who were now taking over the country as if it were their own. He had shown the verses to some close relatives, as well as to a few persons in Morelos who were known for their sympathetic views both to literature and to the old owners of the land. They all had a good laugh over them, and some suggested that they be published, in handbills at least, at one of the printing shops of Morelos. José María had demurred. He did not like the kind of publicity that printing gave. Besides, he did not want the verses to fall into the wrong hands. Some of the landgrabbers had very little sense of humor, as he well knew.

So Don José María did not publish his verses, but he used other methods to make fun of the ragged tramps to their faces. He became their friend. He visited the colony of Los Claveles frequently and talked about the aims of the Revolution with the people there. And it was a rare visit that did not produce its anecdote, to be circulated among the Jiménez tribe amidst merry laughter. A favorite story concerned one Serapio Rendón, a young man whose mother, it was said, was a witch. Don José María had once found Serapio plowing, a six-shooter almost as big as himself strapped about his waist. Don José María called Serapio to the edge of the field.

"Come here, boy," he called. "Come here into the shade, quick! Quick! Before some harm comes to you."

The boy came into the shade quickly enough.

"There," said Don José María with intense relief. "I'm glad I got you out of that sun in time. I would not have answered for your safety much longer."

"Why thank you, Don José María," the boy said. "You are very kind. It is hot enough to give one a fever, is it not?"

"Fever nothing, my boy. It's that enormous cannon you're wearing that worries me. Don't you realize how hot it is? If I hadn't called you out of the sun, that thing would have exploded by now and killed you, perhaps."

"Aw, Don José María! You're joking now."

"Joking? Do you know the boiling point of gunpowder? Answer me that."

"Gee, Don José María, I don't know. I'm not a reading man like you."

"If you won't take it off, and I don't believe you will," Don José María said, "the least you could do is keep it out of the sun."

"That I will do, you can be sure."

And the boy untied his shirttails, let them hang over the pistol to keep it out of the sun, and went back to his plow. Don José María went home laughing.

With their leader, Antonio Cuitla, he amused himself in a different way. The man was an odd conglomeration of quotations from books and tags of ideas picked up from labor agitators. There was no real thought or feeling in the man, but he did like to talk. Don José María would spend hours in Cuitla's *jacal*, wearing his straightest face and talking about the most ridiculous things in the world. And all the time he had to pretend he was drinking the horrible concoction which Cuitla's wife thought was coffee, and which she tried to make attractive by dumping at least a quarter-pound of brown sugar in the cup. Don José María sipped his coffee and let Cuitla talk, merely dropping at intervals a few carefully veiled ironies that were too subtle for Cuitla to understand and

Américo Paredes

which he often took for compliments. Thus he amused himself at Cuitla's *jacal* and also gained thereby. Because after he established himself as a friend and frequent visitor there, no more of his land was affected under the agrarian law.

There was one man in the colony who did not amuse Don José María. His name was Jacinto—*Hyacinth*, of all things. Jacinto del Toro. Del Toro was at the same time too cunning and too ignorant to be flattered: a big black savage, who always scowled at Don José María in a way that betrayed the murderous instincts in his heart. That he might meet Del Toro alone someday, within the limits of the colony or on some lonely road outside, was one of Don José María's most poignant fears. But that was one of the risks he had to take, and he did not stop visiting the colony because of Del Toro, though he often shuddered at the thought that Cuitla might die.

And then the thing happened that he had feared. He sensed it even before he heard the details about it from the people who brought him news in exchange for an *almud* of corn, a can of sardines or an extension of notes overdue. He had sensed it before that day even, in the changed attitude of the rank and file, who no longer listened patiently to his banter, no longer smiled humbly at his thrusts but scowled sullenly when he used them as the butt of his little ironies.

One day, when Don José María arrived at Cuitla's hut, Del Toro was there and got up to go away as he came into the *portal*, brushing his huge bulk against him with purposeful malice and knocking Don José María against the wall. Cuitla did not call Del Toro back, but apologized for him, saying he was unlettered and rude, and then they talked of other things. But when Don José María got up to go, Cuitla became pathetically friendly and pressed his hand several times at parting, and Don José María knew that the time had come to do what must be done.

The Shadow

The problem had developed over the *estero*, that riverbed become a lake which curved around El Carmen de los Jiménez and thrust an arm deep into the agrarian colony of Los Claveles. Del Toro had demanded that the *estero* be drained so they might plant crops on their part of the lake bed. Don José María was opposed. He talked eloquently of water supplies and water tables to them, for he could not talk to them of those other things which made the *estero* dear to him, could not explain to them the link it was, this ex-river, to things that had gone before, to things these newcomer tatterdemalions knew nothing of because they were not made of the same stuff as he. How could one explain to bandits the vision of graceful wharves, of steamers coming upriver in the moonlight? Of romantic girls planning elopements, of colorful Austrian and French uniforms, of battles and horse races and the many bright and splendid things those banks had seen?

So he talked about water tables and half-convinced Antonio Cuitla, who half-understood. And since, to drain the *estero* effectively, the channel which connected it to the river in floodtime must be dammed, a channel that was on Jiménez property, the *estero* was not drained.

It was then that Del Toro began to talk about taking all the land up to the river's edge and driving the landowners out. And the men of the colony, discontent with their high, dry soil, tired of grubbing trunks out of the ground and living in the *jacales* they had made with their own hands, looked greedily at the cleared farms, the neat houses and the planted fields of the people along the river, and they listened to Del Toro.

So Don José María Jiménez had decided that Del Toro must die. For many days he pondered the matter without finding a solution as to the best manner of carrying his decision into effect. His first impulse had been to mount a horse and to ride into the colony and shoot Del Toro down. This plan he had rejected at the last moment as quixotic and improbable of success.

And then, while he wrestled still with the problem, there came to his gate that summer evening, as he sat by his parlor window reading his own verses, the man he had been waiting for.

The dog barked and he looked up and there was the man at the gate, and in that first instant he knew that this was the man. There was something about the way he stood, the manner in which he looked up and down the road and over the gate into the house that told him. He called to the dog and then told the man to come in through the gate.

The man seemed to take a deep breath before he entered, slowly and suspiciously looking from side to side as he walked. Don José María came out to the porch and received him there. He was more of a boy than a man, flat-chested, thin-faced, with a sparse growth of black beard on his face, dressed in city clothes and with worn city shoes on his feet. There was about his whole appearance a sense of pursuit.

"In what way can I serve you, my son?" Don José María asked.

"If you have work," the newcomer said. "Anything that you have to do."

"I have, I have," said Don José María genially, looking into the man's restless eyes.

And he had the man fed in the kitchen and put up for the night in the adobe house that the Jiménezes had built when the lake had been a river.

Chapter 4

Gerardo Salinas was a city boy. The woods frightened him, but he wanted very much to get to Texas. After he slid down from the croup of Don José María's horse, he plunged into the chaparral as one jumping from a great height into darkness.

The deeper he traveled into the brush, the stranger it seemed to him that he should be where he was and not someplace else, almost any other place he could think of. The plaza of his native city, the promenading girls, the serenades, the afternoons in the *cantinas* and the poolrooms—they all came back to him with a surge of nostalgia. He stopped and put out a hand against a tree to steady himself. The trunk he touched was covered with resinous sap. Startled, he snatched away his hand and wiped it against his trousers. The sap from his palm stuck to the cloth, lifting up little hairs when he pulled his hand away. He cursed under his breath and moved on.

He had always been a little boy. Back in the Monterrey *barrio* where he had grown up, he had been known as a pepper pod, little but stinging hot. And thus it happened. Reyes was his friend, but Reyes was drunk and wanted to fight. They threw rocks at each other first and then went on with their knives. Reyes fell back against a nopal plant that grew by the road and the others laughed, drunk as they were. But

Gerardo did not laugh. He got on a bus bound for Nuevo Laredo. And Texas.

He dozed off eventually, and was jerked awake when the bus stopped. Ciudad Victoria, Tamaulipas. He had taken the wrong bus, one going to Tampico and the coast. He tried to remain calm as he got off and took another bus, this one going directly north, toward the river.

The money his mother had given him when she blessed him and kissed him goodbye was not enough for an extra ticket. The second bus took him as far as San Fernando, almost 150 kilometers from his goal. But he was in luck. Some American tourists with fishing gear gave him a ride until they turned off the highway toward the coast.

So he walked, for some twenty kilometers. His narrow dress shoes tortured his feet, but he kept going. Until he reached a ranch by the banks of what he thought was the river, where the old man had guessed his secret. In his face, perhaps, or his walk, or the way he talked.

He felt fortunate indeed. Fate had played with him a bit, but it was now being kind. He would have agreed to anything, just to get across. He accepted the money and the gun. But as he crept toward the tall tree that was his landmark, he did not feel as sure of his destiny as he had half an hour before. It was the last-minute change in plans that bothered him. He did not like it, having to kill two men instead of one.

"He has a small piece of land, with chaparral on three sides," the old man had said. "It will be an easy job."

"How do you know? Have you been there?"

"No, but I have good information about it."

"This one who gave you information, does he know about this too?"

"Him?" The old man laughed. "He's just a fool. He gives me information and thinks we're talking about something else."

"Don't go make a mistake."

"No danger," the man replied. But he added as they reached the little clearing just across the road from the agrarian colony, "You better hurry. He may not be alone for long."

"No?"

"It's almost noon. Somebody will be bringing him his tortillas soon."

"If somebody else is there?"

"You kill them both."

Gerardo hesitated.

"Aren't you man enough?" the old man said.

Gerardo squared his shoulders. "Man enough for three," he said.

But he tried to hurry now, as he went through the brush, nagged by the feeling that he had been cheated.

The heavy automatic felt strange in his hand. He thought that it still smelled of camphor from the trunk where the man got it. The man had shown him how it worked. "Eight shots," the man had said. "Just as fast as you can pull the trigger."

He had stopped a dozen times to make sure the safety catch was on and to worry whether he knew when it was on and when it was off. The fear kept sneaking into his mind, no matter how much he fought to keep it out, that the gun might not fire when he pressed the trigger. And he examined the automatic to see that it was loaded, only to freeze again with dread, lest it go off prematurely and wound him there in the brush all alone.

So he moved toward the spot where this man Del Toro was waiting for him. Impelled by the desire to keep going, to travel in some direction away from the spot where Reyes had died in a pool of blood by the nopal plant, he came to the edge of the brush beside the tall tree and saw through the branches the huge figure of Del Toro, who was plowing his parcel of land.

Gerardo took one look at Del Toro and decided he must leave this man alone. It was not only Del Toro's size, nor the gross face, like one of those stone idols he had seen once, when he visited the capital and went out to look at the relics of the ancient races who had eaten men. There was about Del Toro a ponderous vitality, an immensely powerful force that seemed impossible to kill.

Crouching in the brush close to the tall tree, Gerardo watched the great black man walking after the plow, towering over it so that he seemed to push it along rather than walk behind it. Gerardo held his breath, afraid to move for fear the enormous hulk before him might possess senses in proportion to its size, and that the slightest noise would bring it upon him in his hiding place. He waited for a chance to escape, when Del Toro's plowing would carry him to the other side of the field, as far away as possible.

He had some time to wait, for Del Toro was plowing toward the tree under which Gerardo was in ambush. He came to the edge of the field and turned his team around. As he did so, one of the mules put a hind leg out of the traces. Del Toro boomed out at it in a voice as enormous as himself. The mule shied and stepped back, getting itself entangled in the singletree.

Cursing, Del Toro leaned down and grasped at the mule's fetlock with one great paw while he tried to disentangle the traces with the other. As he bent over, the cartridge belt about his waist slid toward the front until the holstered revolver dangled between his legs. He cursed again and straightened up, stepping away from the kicking mule to jerk the holster behind him. Again he bent over and struggled with the mule, and again the holster slipped forward until it was between his legs.

Del Toro straightened up again, and again he pushed the holster back. He bent over the traces once more, and the holster at once began to follow its stubborn downward path. Gerardo watched, his eyes on the great back now turned to him.

This time Del Toro straightened up with a resolute jerk. He unbuckled the cartridge belt, came up to the tree, a few steps from where Gerardo lay hidden, and carefully deposited pistol and belt at the base of the trunk. Then he turned to the mules again.

At that moment Gerardo knew it was Del Toro's time to die. He stepped out of the brush and fired at Del Toro's back as he squatted beside the mules.

Across the road from the colony of Los Claveles there was in the brush a little depression which after heavy rains became a *resaca*. In drier times it was covered by a rank growth of willow saplings, and it was here that Don José María Jiménez of El Carmen de los Jiménez waited for his hired man. In his pocket were one hundred American dollars in ten-dollar bills.

Some time before, Don José María had watched Gerardo disappear into the brush. As he waited, the scheme that had appeared so perfect the night before began to look less and less probable of success. He remembered how slight a figure Gerardo made and how ferocious Del Toro could be, and he decided he was a fool to hire a little city snotnose for a job like that.

The day before, when Don José María had steered the conversation to Del Toro, Cuitla had mentioned the spot where Del Toro was working.

"It's a sort of out-of-the-way place, isn't it?" Don José María had remarked casually.

Cuitla started, and for a moment Don José María thought he had revealed his plans. But the moment passed, and he had forgotten about it until Gerardo said, "Don't go make a mistake."

Then doubt had come upon Don José María, but too late, and he had got Gerardo to hurry by telling him a lie. No one came to bring a lunch for Del Toro. But for all he knew, his lie was the truth, and Cuitla would visit Del Toro today, and Gerardo would find him there. And perhaps Gerardo would not die, at least not at once.

Then again, for all he knew, he might have underestimated this Cuitla man. Perhaps Cuitla was already there, and Gerardo would find both Del Toro and Cuitla waiting for him. But perhaps Gerardo would get nervous and shoot first. Then they would kill him. A shot in the head perhaps.

The minutes dragged on. Don José María calculated the distance and decided that even if Gerardo had crawled every foot of the way he should have been at Del Toro's plot by now. But no sounds came. There was nothing but the heat and the shimmering, distorted brightness of the day.

Don José María felt like coughing, but any sort of noise might be overheard. He massaged his Adam's apple to ease the tickling in his throat that the thought of coughing had induced, and fought down a desire to clear his throat. Then his horse blew out his breath in a nostril-quivering snort. Don José María started and put his hand to his gun.

And it was then the shots came. One! Two! Three! Then two more in rapid succession. He untied his reins from a willow sapling and waited, one hand on the stirrup flap. Waiting to hear the sound of running feet, the crash of breaking undergrowth as Gerardo Salinas came back.

But nothing happened. He listened intently and heard faint cries and confusion in the distance. Then came several more shots, and after that nothing but silence. Don José

María led his horse through the brush, out onto the road farthest from the colony, and he trotted quietly away.

It was still siesta time when he got home. The yard was deserted. The dog wagged his tail without getting up from where he lay. But his wife was about. Her spare figure came out of the kitchen as he dismounted.

"I'm going across," he told her as he unsaddled. "The back way."

"Yes?"

"I need to see a doctor in Jonesville."

"I see."

"If anybody asks about me, tell them I left early this morning."

Her wrinkled face did not change expression.

"Put a couple of changes of clothes for me in a nosebag. I will get in touch with you."

Gerardo Salinas felt himself the agent of destiny as he raised the automatic and pointed it at Del Toro's back. He no longer was shooting a man for money, for safe passage into Texas. This had become something that had to be, that fate had decreed, when Del Toro disarmed himself and turned back to the mules. Gerardo rose, and taking a step forward into the sun he fired at Del Toro as he squatted behind the mules.

The bullet hit Del Toro squarely in the back, but he did not fall. He sprang erect and turned toward Gerardo, an expression of fierce hatred on his face that was almost delight. Gerardo stood frozen for an instant, as if waiting for Del Toro to come and take the gun away from him. Then he raised the gun again and fired twice more. The bullets slammed into Del Toro's chest at so short a range that bits of his shirt jumped into pieces from the blast.

Américo Paredes

Del Toro had wrapped the reins around his left arm as he struggled with the mules. Now the mules tried to bolt. They pulled the plow forward, jerking Del Toro with them. He fell forward into the furrow he had begun to plow.

Gerardo fired two more times and ran into the brush. Del Toro lay still, his face in the furrow, blackening the plowed earth with his blood.

Gerardo fled into the shady chaparral, his feet heavy and loud as they crashed through the brush, seeking paths that were not there, and as he fled he felt behind him the great black form of Del Toro still in pursuit, still after him with outstretched and clutching hands. He dared not turn to look back for fear that he would see him there, lumbering through the brush behind him, dark and bloody with his outstretched hands.

He blundered through the underbrush, several times coming near the road he had to cross, but zigzagging away from it in his haste. When he finally came upon a road, he saw it was not the right one. He hid there, not far from the edge of it, cowering in a clump of brush for fear of being overtaken. While he was there a flash of bright color caught his eye, and he saw a man wearing a red kerchief riding down the road.

He thought how wonderful it would be to get the man's horse. He could leave the chaparral and ride away down the open road, where nothing could pursue. But the man was armed with a rifle. Gerardo had only the pistol, and he was not close enough to the road.

Then, for the second time that day, fate seemed to beckon to Gerardo Salinas. As the rider came up, the horse reared. The man dismounted and, after studying the dirt in front of him, he walked over to a large ebony close to the road. It was only a matter of creeping forward while the man rested beneath the tree, of getting close enough to make the first shot count.

Gerardo began to move as silently as he could. With the need for silence, the feeling returned that something was at his back, that the bloody thing he had left under another tree had at last caught up with him and was stealthily watching him. But he concentrated on creeping up on the man under the ebony. He was aware that he was making the branches move too much, but the man whose fate it now was to die seemed not to notice. Gerardo crept nearer.

But the horse pointed its ears and he saw the man spring up, heard his voice shouting. Gerardo wanted to raise his pistol and fire. To shout, "Don't shoot! I am your friend!" To come out and give himself up.

But as he hesitated Cuitla fired. He heard the first bullet strike a branch and go whining away. The second one he did not hear. He felt only a blinding pain for an instant, and he was pursued no more.

Chapter 5

After men were dispatched to bury the killer and to take Del Toro home, Cuitla went slowly toward his horse. He unknotted the red kerchief from his throat and thrust it into his pocket as casually as possible, but he noticed that some of the men were staring at him. He did not care. All he wanted was to get home and lie down. He had never felt so tired before. Except once perhaps, long ago, in a mountain pass where he had first seen men killed. He had been excited then, but after the last soldier had been finished off and they were stripping the bodies, he suddenly felt too tired to take part and sat down on a rock to rest. The others had laughed, and the memory of their laughter still stung him. So now he vaulted on his horse as if he were about to lead a charge against some enemy.

"Wait, *jefe*," Juan Sánchez said. "Here are our horses. We will go with you." Some boys were coming across the fields leading a half-dozen horses by the reins.

"We saddled some horses," Serapio Rendón explained, "just in case he broke into the open and we had to run him down."

"You didn't need horses for that," Cuitla said.

He would rather have gone alone and started to say so, but thought better of it. So he waited for them to mount.

"We wouldn't have needed the horses with him on foot," insisted Serapio Rendón. "But he could have got a horse. Now if he had—if you hadn't—if you hadn't shot him just when you did . . ."

He stumbled over his words, not wishing to mention the possibility of Cuitla's death because of the ill luck it still might bring.

"He must have a horse hidden somewhere," another man growled, one of the older ones. "And when we find it, I'll wager whatever you wish it's got the brand of one of the landowners on it."

"If you're coming, come along," Cuitla said. "I'm not going to sit here in the sun all day."

They mounted, Sánchez and Serapio Rendón among them, and rode in a body toward the huts, which were close to the main road. The agrarian colony of Los Claveles lay along one of the roads leading to the city of Morelos. At its back curved the arm of the *estero*, the riverbed turned into a lake. The huts were grouped, village-like, just inside the gate led from the public road.

The land that formed the colony had been pasture land of the Jiménezes and related families, held loosely in common since it had belonged to a common ancestor. For generations cattle and horses had been pastured there by communal agreement, the land being nominally the private property of all of them, so no one had thought to pay taxes. It had been a relatively easy task to dispossess the old communal owners, to make them turn over the land to men working under a different kind of communal arrangement, one backed by a political philosophy the old one had lacked. It had been almost too easy, and sometimes Cuitla, because of his friendship with Don José María Jiménez, felt twinges of conscience.

But after all, as Cuitla had told himself countless times, they had left the best land, the riverbank land, to the old families. They had taken the poorest land, which was lying unused, pasturing only a few horses and cows when human beings could raise corn and beans and cotton on it. Surely it was not too much to ask for a share of what belonged in truth to all of them. But the landowners for the most part had not been sympathetic. There were very few of them like Don José María, who understood the agrarian law and wanted to see the peon rise and become a man.

Curse these rich men! And Del Toro too, with his thirst for more and more land. More and more trouble. More and more blood. Cuitla shook his head. He did not want to think about Del Toro now.

But the men would not let him forget. They were talking about Del Toro as they rode along, surrounding Cuitla protectively, forming a bodyguard about him to shield him from other killers who might be lurking in the brush.

"It's a good thing we still have the *presidente* with us," one of them said.

"An act of Providence," said another.

"But we will miss the Chief of the Rural Police," said a third.

"A man like him is not easily replaced."

They rode in silence for a while, and then the first man said, "Well, at least we don't have to go far to know who did it."

"Sure. They were afraid of him."

"He made things too hot for them, that was why. They were afraid he would take more of their precious lands, that they want to pasture rabbits in."

"Comrade," the first man said, "he died for all of us. This will not stay the way it is for long."

"Stop talking nonsense!" Cuitla said. "Here you are, working yourselves up to go kill somebody, to start trouble when you should be starting a crop. And you don't even know who killed Del Toro or why."

"Does it take a lot to guess?" Juan Sánchez asked softly.

"Perhaps more than you think," Cuitla said, turning in his saddle to stare at Sánchez. "How do you know this man came from one of the landowners? Is there any proof? Do you think Del Toro had no other enemies but these people here? You didn't know him the way I did."

They were silent for a while and Cuitla hoped he had put a doubt in their minds. There was no doubt in his own mind where the killer had come from. But he must keep them quiet and working the land.

"The thing," one of the men said, "is to make sure exactly who it was who hired this city man."

"It could have been any one of them," said another. "They all hated him. They were all afraid of him."

"What's the name of this one who always visits the colony?"

"Oh, no!" Juan Sánchez said. "It could not be him. Why, he's the *presidente's* friend!"

Serapio Rendón said, "The man who did this was no friend of anyone here, least of all the *presidente*. That man was out to kill them both. It is a miracle that we did not lose both of them, our best men, at one blow."

"You are wrong," Cuitla said gently, for he liked Serapio Rendón. "You are wrong. The city man was not after me. It was an accident that we met."

It could not have been possible for the outsider to know he was going to ride down that wagon trail on that particular day. And the killer had gotten his chance when Cuitla stopped under the tree. It had been an accident, right after the outsider had done Cuitla a great favor. For after all, killing a man you had known and fought beside—it would not have been an easy thing to do.

"No," Cuitla told himself. "The city man did not know that we would meet." Then it suddenly occurred to him. "But *he* would have known. *He* knew and he was warning me. He knew I was about to pass the spot where the outsider was hiding. And so soon after death he did not know. We had been such good friends always."

Cuitla checked himself abruptly. He was an emancipated man, free in body and mind, no slave to either master or priest. He did not believe in those dark things that haunted his men's minds. He had cast such things away as he had thrown aside the round straw hat and the cotton drawers. But sometimes, from living too much with them, one got into their habit of mind, even though one did not believe.

Still, he would have liked to talk about these things to someone who understood, someone who appreciated the way he felt. Someone like Don José María. There was a man who understood. How often had he wished that life had been different, and that Don José María and he had been born in the same village. Or that he, Antonio Cuitla, had been born a riverbank man.

He would like to sit down with Don José María over a cup of coffee and say, "What do you think, Don José María? Supposing that there were such a thing as life after death, just supposing such a thing were true, and that the soul remained itself. What do you suppose a man would do—a soul—who had just died if a friend whose heart . . . "

He brought himself up short, and the daydream evaporated in the heat of his self-scorn. But the thought of Don José María reminded him of an urgent matter. The risks any landowner would take if he came into the colony just now. He must send someone to El Carmen as soon as he got home.

"He must have taken off his pistol belt right before it happened," Juan Sánchez was saying. "He put it right there under the tree and handed himself over to the killer. The signs were clear. But why he did it we'll never know, unless his ghost comes back and tells us about it."

The others laughed uneasily, and Cuitla frowned.

"It was his time to die," said a thin, long-necked man named Lupe Melguizo, who was riding close to Cuitla. "It just happened to be his time, and when it is your time to die, you die. Your own blood chokes you in your throat, seeking to come out of you. That's why Del Toro did it. It was his time to die."

"That is true," Sánchez said. "There is such a thing as one's time, whatever people say." He glanced sideways at Cuitla, who ignored him. "It was Del Toro's time, while the *presidente*'s has not yet come. May it not come for many years."

The others added their murmurs of assent. Cuitla bowed his head and smiled.

"When one's time comes, it comes. There is nothing one can do about it," Sánchez continued. "Now, when one knows, as sometimes happens—"

"Your time has certainly held off, old man," interrupted one of the men, and the rest laughed. Even Cuitla smiled a faint smile, and the men laughed again.

"Yes," Sánchez said. "My time has not yet come, and I may die in bed of chills and fever, for all I know. But when it does come, I will not fight against it, for I know it does no good. That is, if I am allowed to know. Some people"—he glanced at Cuitla again—"some people are told the future, but it does them no good. There was the king who was told his son would die on the horns of a bull. They took the boy to the city and would not let him ride a horse or join the vaqueros in roping and tailing steers. And one day he was out walking and stumbled on an old skull with the horns still on it, and he fell down and the horns pierced his side. A man's lot is his lot."

The others clucked their tongues. Cuitla scowled and was silent. He was trying to figure how long it had taken the city man to travel from where he had killed Del Toro. It would not have been long; Del Toro's body must have still been warm.

How long did life remain in a body after a fatal wound? How long did the soul—if it did exist—how long did it hover over the body, or whatever it was that made up life? It could not have been long. Del Toro's body was still warm, his blood still hot from the effort and the pain he suffered when he died.

Cuitla closed his eyes again, rocking along for a few moments through the red darkness behind his eyelids. When he opened them again, Sánchez, who was riding on his right, was looking at him. He became aware that a question had been asked of him and was startled like a man awakened from sleep.

Serapio Rendón, riding on Cuitla's left, repeated his question. "How was it, *jefe*," he said, "that you saw the stranger first? I have been turning it over and over in my head just now, how you were able to see him in the brush and you on horseback in the road."

"I had dismounted," Cuitla said. "I . . . I saw something on the road and . . ." He checked himself in time.

Serapio's eyes grew round. "You saw something?"

"It was nothing. I saw something. That is, at least I thought I had. I dismounted to look for tracks."

There was a knowing, almost professional briskness in Sánchez's voice. "This something, chief. What did it look like?"

Américo Paredes

"What did what look like! Has anyone ever seen such fools as all of you! I told you I saw some tracks, or rather I thought I saw them and dismounted to look. They looked so from horseback. But there was nothing on the road, nothing. There were no tracks there. And when I saw that I had been mistaken, I walked over to the ebony. The cinch was loose," he explained, feeling as he did so that it would be much better to say the least possible. But he went on. "The cinch was loose and I noticed it when I dismounted. So I went to the ebony, I went to tighten it. I didn't want to stand in the hot sun, in the middle of the road, while I tightened it, when I could do it in the shade. There is a good shade there, under that ebony, a very good shade."

"Yes," Sánchez said, "there is good shade there."

"Very good, very good shade," Cuitla said.

"And there were no tracks," Sánchez said. "There on the road."

"I told you there were not!"

"A premonition," Sánchez said, in the tone of a doctor diagnosing a case.

Cuitla snorted. "If anyone had a premonition," he said lightly, "it was this sorrel of mine."

And he patted the sorrel's neck while he told them how the horse had pointed its ears at the stranger. Serapio Rendón listened eagerly, leaning forward in his saddle to catch every word. He was a round-faced young man, the son of one of Cuitla's men who had died in revolutionary times. A young man with quick tawny eyes and a curious mind. A good boy, this Serapio. Cuitla liked him even though he was the healing woman's son.

"He was trying to tell you," Serapio said abruptly. "He was trying to warn you, he wanted you to know the man was there."

"Who?"

"The horse, *jefe*," Serapio said. "He knew the city man was there and he was trying to tell you by pointing his ears. Some horses are like Christians, only they can't talk."

"Oh," Cuitla said.

They rode in silence after that, until they reached the village. He knew the men were looking at him and exchanging glances among themselves.

Chapter 6

The news had preceded them and women were wailing in Del Toro's hut. They would be at it all night, howling as if Del Toro's death had been the greatest possible personal loss to each one of them. Like savages, Cuitla thought. But there were some customs he could not break them of. The moans rose and fell, some voices crying in a higher pitch, others in a lower, and then changing places in dreary counterpoint.

Cuitla rode towards his own hut while the men dismounted before Del Toro's. Oh, yes, Del Toro's wife could wail. Del Toro had been good, he had been gentle. When he beat her, he had been careful not to break her ribs. Or her nose.

In a while the women would be tired, and they would stop and spend some time gossiping and laughing. Until they were rested up, when they would yell again as if they would die of grief. It was all false, but required. Like the priest at mass, raising that shiny gold thing at the congregation and saying to himself as he drank the wine, "To the health of all you *pendejos.*"

Cuitla grinned. He had heard that joke in Texas in his youth, and it was one of his favorites. He liked to tell it to his men, just to test them, but it never failed to shock the women. That was how they were made. They required the foolishness, the dupery, even more than the men.

He dismounted in front of his own hut, which stood facing the gate leading to the public road. His little boy, admiring eyes upon his father, came running out and took the horse.

"Give him a handful of corn," Cuitla told his son. He thought a moment. "Give him two handfuls."

The boy nodded excitedly and led the horse away as Cuitla walked into his hut. It was by far the best *jacal* in the village. He had been careful to make it tall, neat and roomy. Some of the other huts were built so low that a man almost had to squat to go in the door. Just dens and nothing more. But one had to advance by degrees.

The roof of Cuitla's hut was so high that a man barely had to duck his head to go in the door. It was neatly thatched with *zacahuiste* grass, and the walls were so well daubed with clay that their wooden skeleton did not show at all.

Cuitla crossed under the portico that served the hut as a gallery, a shade constructed of four saplings thatched with bamboo, and entered the smoky interior. His wife was at the other end, bending over a fireplace made of mud and sticks, like the hut itself, and, like it, carefully and neatly built.

She turned quickly when she heard him enter, her mouth open, her eyes wide and her breath coming quickly. For a moment he thought she would embrace him and start screaming.

"It's all right," he said. "Everything's all right." He tried to speak softly, gently, but his voice came out weary and bored.

"I was not sure it had not been you," she said. "I could not be sure until I saw you with my own eyes."

Cuitla hung his hat on a peg in the wall. "Well, you can see now it wasn't me," he said. He sat down beside the table, leaning his arm on it. His wife gave him a soft, patient look. She lifted the front of her dirty black skirt slightly and wiped her hands, still looking at him with her big, sad eyes. Her eyes were so big and alive that they did not seem to belong in her old ugly face. She seemed to be looking at him from *behind* her face, and it startled him.

He turned away and said irritably, "Where is that boy? Why does he always loiter when I send him somewhere?"

She looked out the window and replied, "He is coming now. He's on his way back from the shed."

He remained with his back to her, his elbows on the table, his chin in his hands, not wanting to look at her, this strange woman hiding behind a face.

Yet, she had been his woman for more than fifteen years. After a battle, a town, a drunken spree such as he had loved in his younger days. The next morning she had been walking behind him, and from then on she had made his tortillas and brought his food hot to him, in camp and in battle, faithful ever since. The times had been hard. Sitting there with his elbows on the table, he remembered the children she had borne him in those days when she had been his *soldadera*, his soldier woman and not his wife. The children had all died. Cold perhaps, hunger, disease. Only this boy, the child of their middle age, born fortunately, when the hardships of campaigning were over, when she could have at least a permanent corner in some barracks rather than the endless marches after the column as in former days.

A priest had told her that God spared this last of her children because he had been born in wedlock, while the others were not. God had punished them because she had been his whore, the priest had said. Cuitla had wanted to kill the priest, but she would not let him do it. Perhaps it had been just as well. It was the same priest who had married them. She had wanted to be married, and he gave in to her whim.

But he had wanted to kill the priest then, though he did not like to kill men like that.

He jerked his head up impatiently. His son was standing before him, very straight, his arms folded and waiting to be spoken to, as he had been taught.

"Is the pinto mare at hand?" Cuitla asked.

"Yes, father. She is tied to the shed."

"Good." He reached up to the ledge under the eaves and took down an indelible pencil and a note tablet, to write Don José María Jiménez. But once he brought the pencil to rest over the paper, he was overcome by indecision. The words that came to his mind sounded strange to him. He was also in doubt as to how much he should say. It was not the same as talking to a friend face to face. At last he decided to write a short note, merely stating that something had happened at the colony, and that Don José María had better stay away until Cuitla came to explain.

Several times he tore sheets to fragments and threw them into the fire. He grew dissatisfied with his way of saying things and agonized over whether *haber* took a *v* or a *b*. His ornamented handwriting, of which he was so proud, now made him ashamed. At last he set down a note, heedless of spelling and calligraphy, a short note that sounded cold and formal when he reread it. He sealed it and gave it to his son.

"It must be delivered into Don José María's hands, into his hands alone."

"To no one else?"

"To no one else. Now go. God speed you."

The boy hurried out and Cuitla turned back to the table, smiling. There it was. It was so hard to get rid of those things, even in himself. But those were merely words. Once a man had told him that *ojalá* meant "If Allah wills." Everyone said it, even the priests. There was no meaning to words like that. Still, he wished he could rid his language of them.

His wife saw him smiling. She stared at him from across the room and shook her head. Then she turned back to the fireplace and deftly turned over a tortilla on the flat piece of iron that served as a griddle.

He sat there for a long time, trying not to think about anything at all. The mourning for Del Toro was still going on. The moans were easier to bear. They came and went in a dull monotone that fitted well into Cuitla's state of mind. But the screams were another thing. They jabbed at him like the point of a knife.

"They have to put on their little act," he told his wife. She was back at the chimney and looked at him over her shoulder. "Yes," he said. "You tell me what makes them act the way they do."

"I don't know," she said.

"Do you want to go out there with them too? Why aren't you with them? Why don't you go and scream for a while? It would do you good, would it not?"

"Do you want me to go?"

"I don't give a damn."

"I don't want to go," she said.

He dropped his head upon his fist, but a scream from Del Toro's hut jerked him upright. "Savages!"

"They cry because he is dead. It is the custom."

"Are they sad because the son-of-a-bitch is dead?"

"No matter what kind of man he was, one must respect his ghost."

"Ghost! He has no ghost! He is dead, he is dirt. Like a horse or a dog. Don't talk to me about ghosts, you fool."

She folded her hands in front of her skirt. "I did not mean it like that," she said. "Perhaps there is nothing, like you say.

You know more than I do. But one must show respect. After all, he was your friend. For many years he was your friend."

For a while he did not reply. When he spoke at last, it was in a quieter voice. "Tend to your cooking," he said.

He would not listen to them. He had better things to do. Anyway, it had all been a stupid mistake. And after all, whatever he might have intended, he had done nothing at all. But the intent is itself a sin, the priests would say. Well, he knew a joke about that too . . .

There was another scream, louder and more outraged than all the others that had gone before. He sprang up and began to pace back and forth.

It was his own mother who was screaming as she knelt on the floor of the hut, a tuft of her gray hair in one of her fists, her other hand beating her withered Indian face while she screamed and screamed. And little Antonio crouched in a corner, an unbearable sense of anguish struggling with shame for his mother, hitting her head on the dirt floor in front of the corpse of his father, the man with shoes and Spanish blood just brought in from the *cantina* covered with blood and dirt.

Now there was no screaming. His mother squatted yet before the body, while the candles burned. She and the other crones laughed and joked and gossiped. Antonio's father lay there, his father who would never speak to him again, never joke again, never tell him about that city in the north where he had been born. He lay there, his mouth saying nothing, his ears deaf both to the wails and the laughter. And the little boy crept away, no longer wanting to see what was once his father. Outside, the anguish was gone, swallowed in burning shame and disgust, a disgust that had stayed with him ever since.

Cuitla paced the length of his hut. "Savages!" he muttered. "Savages!"

Then all the voices screamed at once, as if they did not care for anything at all except tearing out the burning grief from within them.

Cuitla rushed to the door. "Silence!" he yelled. "Silence! Silence!"

They had just brought Del Toro's body home. Four men were struggling through the doorway with the huge lump. It lay on a rude stretcher, covered with burlap sacking, like a large bale being carried in from the rain.

The screams rose higher and higher. Cuitla flung himself out of his hut and strode across the bare, hard-packed ground. He stood in the doorway of Del Toro's hut, his fists clenched. "Silence!" he yelled. "You will be silent!"

The screams stopped abruptly. Del Toro's wife stared at him, her hands tangled in her hair, her wet face trembling.

Cuitla cried shrilly, "Animals! You will not scream again! I order it!"

Del Toro's wife looked at him as if he had struck her. Then she began to sob quietly, biting at her hand, still looking at him with hurt upon her face. The other wild, disarranged women gathered about her, soothing her, making little noises as one makes to babies. He turned away, and the mourning continued in a muffled key.

The men who had brought Del Toro's body home gathered about the entrance and looked at his receding back.

Juan Sánchez said, "It has been a very difficult day."

Once more in his hut, Cuitla tried to eat his supper. He pushed the plate of beans and stewed rabbit aside after a few mouthfuls.

"Give me the bottle," he told his wife.

"The bottle?"

"The mezcal bottle. I will have a drink."

She went and got it from the corner shelf where she kept her spoons and dishes. They kept it as medicine because he had stopped drinking for pleasure many years ago. Now he took a swallow, then another, and still a third. The liquor seemed to vaporize in his breast, to seep through all his ribs and into his shoulders, arms and back.

After a few more drinks, he set himself to eat with appetite, looking up from his plate just once, to inquire whether that boy had come back from his errand.

Chapter 7

After supper, they brought him the stranger's belongings. Cuitla put them on the table before him: a watch, the pistol, some money, a wallet and a few other odds and ends. Cuitla looked through the wallet for some identifying paper, dreading to find it but looking nevertheless. He found none.

He was sorting out the stranger's things when he heard the soft thud of hoofs on the dirt outside. His son had arrived and was leading the mare to the shed. In a moment the boy appeared at the door. His dark face was ashy, his eyes larger than usual. He stood in the doorway in the light of the kerosene wick, breathing heavily, obviously making an effort to catch his breath.

"What's the matter?" Cuitla demanded.

"I . . . I . . ." the boy began, his eyes growing wider in his effort to talk. Then he stopped to take a deep breath. His face assumed a guarded, formal expression. "I'm sorry I'm late," he said with just a slight tremor in his voice. "I had to wait for him a long time."

"He was not there?"

"No. When I got to El Carmen, they said he was out for a moment and would I leave the message and that they would give it to him. But you had told me to give it to him and no one else."

Cuitla nodded his approval.

"So I told them I'd wait. They brought me a cup of coffee and I sat on the steps until it got dark."

"You gave it to him then, and what did he say?"

"No. I did not do so. I waited until dark, but he never showed up."

"Why didn't you ask them where he was?"

"I didn't think I should. They walked about as if they did not want to see me."

Cuitla pressed his lips together impatiently.

"At last, the lady of the house came out and talked to me. She said that Don José María had left for Jonesville this morning. So I did not give the letter to anyone. Here it is."

Cuitla took the letter. "You acted well," he said. "You did well in bringing the letter back to me."

The boy's face brightened.

"You must tell no one about this letter."

The boy nodded.

"Go eat your supper."

Cuitla took the letter to the chimney, dropped it on the coals and watched it burn. After it had turned black, he poked at it with a stick until the ashes became a powder. He sat down again, opposite his son, elbows on the table and chin in his hands, glancing now at the stranger's belongings, now at his son.

For a while Cuitla watched his son eat. Then he opened the stranger's wallet and spread the contents out on the table again. The boy's errand had told him more than he would find here. But there was no clear proof, no way to know.

The boy rose from the table and went to squat by the doorway, looking out into the dark. "What are you staring at?" his father said. "Don't you have anything else to do?"

The boy moved away from the door to a spot just beside it, sitting down on a piece of log there. He took a half-finished quirt from under his blouse and began to plait the rawhide thongs. But his fingers trembled, and he merely acted as if he were plaiting, without accomplishing anything but fumbling at the thongs. Cuitla turned back to the things on the table.

It was a brand-new wallet of tooled leather that had not known sweat in its owner's pocket. But some of the things in it had been in another wallet. There was no name. Cuitla had expected that. Besides a few Mexican bills, there was the photo of a girl; a guitar string still neatly wound inside its transparent envelope; a small medallion attached to one pink bead, part of a rosary perhaps; and a clipping from a Mexican newspaper. The clipping was about the coming cotton season in Texas and the need for pickers, the high wages being offered. An advertisement. Cuitla put it down and looked at the photograph of the girl. It was a cheap print, already yellow, although the paper did not look old. A young girl with a pale face and abundant dark hair, with large eyes and a pouting mouth. There was nothing written on the back.

Cuitla sighed and put the articles back in the wallet, thinking not about the young stranger who had killed Del Toro, but of himself. He, too, had gone to Texas when he was young, after his father died and he ran away for the first time from the village where he was born.

That was long ago. But he had carried among his effects much the same things. No gun. It was later that he had learned to use one. But much the same other junk, except the guitar string and the medallion. He had never been good at music, that was one of the things that had set him apart from most of the young men of the village, who sang and played and danced. Too serious, his mother had said. Too sour, more than one girl remarked, enviously perhaps. Because he was different.

Américo Paredes

He had not carried a medallion either. He had been different in that way too, proud and cynical so that the others called him atheist and were afraid of him. He had not carried a medallion to Texas, but he had taken many ignorant ideas that he had gotten rid of since. It was in Texas he first heard men talk of revolution, men of his own sort, talk about striking off their chains, and of the imprisonment of starvation. Yes, he had got most of his education in Texas. In the cotton fields and the coal mines.

And Del Toro, too. He also received his education there, especially at the Huntsville prison farm. Texas had a lot to teach the Mexican peon turned migrant laborer, who looked across the border for a new kind of life. But this young stranger had never reached the promised land, fleeing as he had been. From what, God only knew.

He stopped, realizing that in spite of all his resolve his thoughts had again described a straggling circle and come back to the same things: Del Toro and God. He grinned crookedly. He had killed God long ago. Now Del Toro was gone, and he was sure that neither of them existed any more.

But the important thing was the land, to keep the men working until the corn was tall, until the white cotton burst open in the boll. That time would quickly come, the dream would be. Men did not matter of themselves as long as the land gave fruit.

He was not aware of his wife's approach until she spoke suddenly at his shoulder. "Are you going to the wake?"

"The wake?" he said distantly, his mind slowly drifting back. "The wake?"

"You are going, are you not?"

He did not answer.

"You must go," she said. He shook his head.

"It is your duty," she told him. "You are the president. You must go."

"All right," he said with a sigh of resignation.

He remained where he was, with his elbows on the table, and she put her hand timidly on his shoulder, smoothing away at a wrinkle in his shirt.

"What is it?" she asked. "What is it?"

A warm feeling came upon him with a rush, almost drowning him. He turned toward her, on the brink of the words he was trying so hard to keep to himself. He opened his mouth as if to speak and stopped. She looked down at him calmly.

"Nothing," he said roughly. He brushed her hand away from his shoulder and got up. "Put those things away," he said and walked toward the door.

His little boy still sat by the doorway, half crouching and still making believe that he plaited a quirt while he watched his father with his big, frightened eyes. He moved out of the way, still squatting. Cuitla stopped and looked down at him.

"Why aren't you out with the other children?"

The boy looked up at his father. "I . . . I . . . ." He paused. "I'm all right here."

"You should go out and play, not skulk in corners. Out with you!"

The boy stirred without moving from the same spot. "I don't want to go," he said. "I'm afraid."

"Afraid?"

"You will say it didn't," the child said, "but it did happen. I *did* see it."

"See what?" his mother said.

"On the road, something on the road the way back. A lump in the dark that ran and frightened the mare. I saw it, I swear."

"You are a fool!" his father said.

Américo Paredes

"Don't be so hard on him," his mother said. "There must have been something. Some animal, a coyote perhaps. Please let him be."

Cuitla did not reply. He crossed over to Del Toro's hut. The men were squatting along the wall outside. Vague, blurry forms they were, lumps of darker darkness in the blackness of the night. They were talking in low tones and passing bottles from hand to hand in the dark. It was part of the ceremony of the wake, the talk and the drinking, and though Cuitla did not allow drinking in the colony, he knew he could not prevent it at this time.

But at least he could keep it from appearing too public. He made his presence known by clearing his throat, and the bottles were put away. For the remainder of his visit the bottles did not reappear, though men were constantly going off into the farther darkness, silently in twos and threes, and returning just as silently to take their places in the line of dark squatting forms along the shadow of the hut.

Cuitla went up to the doorway and looked in. They had laid straw mats on the dirt floor, and on these rested the enormous mass that had been Del Toro, with his hands over his great belly, as if he were asleep. The blood of his wounds had been washed away. Candles had been lighted, yellow wax candles adorned with shiny tinfoil bands, like those of big cigars, expensive wax candles bought at the stores of Morelos and carefully treasured by the women of Los Claveles for occasions such as this. Two of them had been lighted at the head, two at the feet. Someone had made a cross out of two small pieces of mesquite tied together with *pita* thongs, and it had been put into Del Toro's folded hands. Around the corpse knelt black-clad women, their bare feet folded behind them, rosaries in their hands, muttering prayers in a ceaseless, bodiless hum.

He did not go in. A chair was brought for him, and he sat down among the men, who squatted about him. He sat as on a throne, looking over their shadowy heads. After he had settled down, the conversation, which his coming had interrupted, was resumed. The talk was in low murmurs. It came and went in little eddies with lulls in between, swirling about small groups of men, never general, sleepy talk interspersed here and there with chuckles as someone told a joke.

From where he sat, Cuitla could look in and see the body, the lighted candles and the women, and during the lulls in the men's talk he heard the monotonous murmur of the prayers. He smiled, sitting there in the dark, surrounded by his men, who with their little conversations, their jokes and their drinking were carrying out their part in the ritual of the wake. The opium of the people.

He remembered he had told them that once, and they had listened open-mouthed as he harangued them, drinking in every word he said, cheering him at the end as he stood triumphantly among them, feeling that at last he had stirred them, at last opened their eyes, made them see through their ignorance. He had felt that he was witnessing a birth. Only later did it occur to him that not one of them knew what opium was. He could have said the mezcal of the people, and they would have understood. Only it would not have had the same effect. They would not have cheered him then. For to them, mezcal was good. They would not have liked "the mezcal of the people." Opium was the right word, the magic word, because they had not understood. And that was what they liked best, the things they could not understand.

It had all been fine, wonderful, fine and progressive. They had liked it all. But they knew what they wanted, and it now was much clearer to him than it ever had been, sitting here within a pebble's throw of Del Toro's mortal remains. The mezcal, the wakes and the screaming: They wanted them as much as the land, perhaps even more. They could pillage the churches and cross themselves while doing so. Kill the priests but save the opium. That was it.

Once he had seen Del Toro kill a priest. They were riding a train as part of the guard through *Cristero* country, the same country Del Toro had lived in before the agrarian *Cristero* wars had driven him out. They puffed around a hill and found the track torn out, and when they stopped the *Cristeros* had attacked the train, shouting "Long live Christ the King!"

There was a troop of regular soldiers forward and Cuitla's irregulars in the rear. The *Cristeros* had not expected that. While the troops engaged them on the track, Cuitla and his men had cut behind. They came upon their rear and there in a little hollow was the priest, directing the attack. The priest tried to run when he saw them, but he tripped in his cassock. Del Toro shot him and the priest fell, kicking like a rabbit. Del Toro took out his machete and ran toward him, shouting joyfully, "Got him! Got him!"

A *Cristero* came up behind Del Toro and made a tremendous pass at his head with a machete, while Cuitla, afraid to shoot, shouted helplessly. The blow sliced through the wide brim of Del Toro's hat and the big man turned and cut the *Cristero* down. He came back grinning after finishing off the priest.

"That was a close one," Cuitla said.

Del Toro paused to pick his big flat nose. "God," he said, flicking away a gob of dried snot, "guarded my back."

In all the memories he could call back just now, he saw Del Toro killing someone. A jovial man, really, but there were times when he grew restless and ugly, when he had to have his drink of blood, after which his whole being seemed replenished. Until the next time. This time it had been Del Toro's turn.

But then there rose to reproach him the vision of Del Toro shooting a path out of his native village through a ring of the soldiers of Christ. Del Toro, young and slim and quick, his pistol in his hand, the only man in the village left alive, killing his way to freedom, but leaving his brother dead, and his sister and his sweetheart to be raped before they died.

And then Cuitla saw in his mind's eye the *Cristeros* not as he remembered them, but instead as men with two enormous crucifixes, two great big crosses on chains, one hanging in front and one in back, and they were running around killing people and raping women and kissing the crucifixes all the while, first the one in front and then the one in back, all at one and the same time, before they killed and when they wiped their blades, before they threw a woman to the ground and as they got up after raping her.

He smiled. That was one of Don José María's humorous descriptions of the *Cristeros*, one which had won him the sympathies of many in the colony. He pushed the memory of Don José María out of his mind, in part at least so that it stood at a distance, where it became intermingled with that of Del Toro.

Friendship? A breath that the wind takes away. The great reality was the land. He became aware that one of the men was standing close to his chair and was speaking to him.

"Yes?" he said. "Yes?"

The man repeated his question. Did the *presidente* wish to see the body now?

"Later," he said and the man went away.

Américo Paredes

Those in the dark about him were muttering. Their talk had become organized and purposeful. Someone raised his voice: "Well, is there anybody who thinks different?"

Cuitla pretended not to hear. Another man cleared his throat. Then a third asked him directly, "Is it true, *jefe?*"

There was a moment's silence before Cuitla's quiet voice said, "What is true?"

"That you . . ." the man began. "That you found no signs."

"None to show who sent him."

Another voice broke in, a frank youthful voice. "*Jefe*, is it true what we hear? That Don José María has gone to the other side of the river?"

"So I hear," Cuitla said. "He left early this morning, I am told."

"How do we know that's the truth?" said another voice.

"Are you saying that I lie?" Cuitla said.

There was a silence. Finally one man spoke. "We mean no harm," he said. "Only that we want to know. We want to even things up, which is natural, isn't it?"

Many voices joined in. "Things just can't stay like this. Someone has got to pay. Right, by God, they'll pay."

They were talking very low because of the corpse, and Cuitla could only guess at their voices. "The trouble with all of you," he said, "is that you don't like to work. You've got the land you wanted, and all you think about is shooting, excitement. Anything but buckling down to work."

"But a comrade has been killed," the voices muttered. "The Chief of the Rural Police."

There was no police force in the colony, but Del Toro had wanted a title too, so he made one up for himself. The voices in the dark were hissing and muttering in a higher key. "Kill them!" they said. "Kill them all! Drive them out! Burn their houses and drive them out!"

"Here! Here!" Cuitla raised his voice. They stopped talking, expectant. "There will be no shooting. I am still in command here."

The men stirred, then were still. "The Revolution is over," Cuitla went on. "Can't you understand that? We must work the land."

"And Del Toro?" one of the voices asked.

"The outsider killed Del Toro. I myself took care of the outsider. What more do you want?"

The men said nothing.

"We'll call the general from Morelos to investigate," he added, "to find out who sent the outsider. And the guilty will be punished according to the law."

"I wonder if one of my woman's skirts will fit me," said a voice in the dark.

"What was that?" Cuitla said, leaning forward in his chair.

The titter was choked at its inception. No one replied, and he thought it best to let the matter pass. Cuitla rose, feeling their eyes upon him as he stood in the light of the doorway.

"I will see him now," he said.

Del Toro's wife met him at the door. He gave her his condolences, as if nothing had happened that afternoon. She received his words with simple dignity and beckoned him in. He went up to the body and looked it in the face.

It surprised him just a bit that the face was just a face like all other dead faces. There was nothing remarkable about it. It was just a dead face. He had seen many faces like that before, more than he would care to remember. There was nothing uncommon about the face of a dead man. If one was young and green, such a sight could make one sick, especially if it was a freshly killed corpse with all its features disarranged. But this one had been washed and put in order. It was all in order, this dead face. He squatted down before it.

It was just a hunk of black mud, beginning to stink already. A bloated, evil face. The eyes swollen and shut. Couldn't see anything. Nor know anything at all. He felt a cold, dropping sensation inside.

He clenched his teeth and scowled down at the dead face. At the hands that held their rude crucifix in a gentle clasp.

He would touch one of the hands. He would pass his fingers over it, just the tips of his fingers, ruffling the hairs on the back of it, just as he had often done with the hide of a deer or some other animal he had killed. He put out his hand.

The face below him blurred and he withdrew his hand to steady himself. Del Toro's wife was looking at him. He put out his hand again over the dead face, as if to brush it with his fingers. His hand began to shake. He tried to stop it, but by that time his arm was shaking too, and then all of him was shaking.

He sprang to his feet and stumbled out of the hut, walking away in long swift strides. He did not stop until he reached his own hut. In its shadow he turned to look back. Del Toro's wife was standing in the doorway, still looking after him. In the quietness he could make out the voices of the men, talking in low tones again, as they sat huddled in little groups in the black night.

Chapter 8

The light was out in his hut. Cuitla groped his way inside and placed a low lattice made of sticks across the doorway, to keep dogs out during the night. That was the one thing he feared intensely, rabid dogs. The thought that a mad animal might come upon him while sleeping and take him by the throat terrified him. In his franker moments he admitted to himself that this fear, which few others in the colony shared, was also a relic of his early years, born of tales he had heard in his village. But at least it was a reasonable fear. Dogs were flesh and blood, and their teeth were real. Rabies was a terrible disease for which there was no cure.

He made sure the lattice was in place firmly enough to resist the weight of a large dog if it threw itself against the framework. Satisfied, he went to bed. The bed was nothing but a blanket-covered pallet laid on a platform of willow saplings, but it was a bed, and it kept him above the dust and fleas. He had set himself to making it almost as soon as he had finished the hut, constructing the frame out of saplings and the top from packing-case boards, the whole structure put together with rawhide thongs instead of nails. The rest of the colony slept on pallets, thrown on the ground at night and rolled up in the morning.

Away from the doorway, his feet groped out a circular path because his son slept on the ground by the door. But when he reached the edge of the bed, he looked back and could see the doorway outlined against the lesser dark outside. His son was not there.

"Where is he?" he demanded.

"He's—he's at a friend's house," his wife answered.

"This late?"

He eased himself down and groped at one of his shoes. The bed would be a welcome blessing tonight. He worked on the shoe for a moment, fumbling blindly. Then he stopped and turned toward her.

"Where is he?"

She did not reply.

"Where is he staying?"

"With Serapio Rendón."

"At the healing woman's!"

"Don't be angry. You saw how frightened he was."

"Why should he be frightened?"

"Please try to understand. We were all frightened about what happened this afternoon. And when they started saying that it had been you . . ."

"Me? What do you mean me?"

"That it had been you and not Del Toro the stranger shot."

"Oh," he said.

"That was enough to upset anyone. It affected him very much. He loves you. He admires you. He is a sensitive boy."

"Men should not be sensitive," Cuitla said, in a gentler tone.

"So when you sent him on that errand, he was frightened already. Then an animal started under his horse's feet, and it made the matter worse. I could tell—he *had* to see the healing woman. Things like that have to be cured immediately, or they can become incurable."

"Spirits! Rag dolls pierced with pins! Prayers! Spells!"

"There is no need to get angry. She'll cure him overnight."

"Agh!" Cuitla said to the darkness. "What can one do with them?"

"It's just a case of simple fright sickness," his wife said. "It happens to everybody at one time or another."

"Just a case of simple fright sickness," he mimicked.

She was silent for a brief moment and then said in a soft voice that had just a hint of coyness in it, "You were cured of it yourself once. Do you remember? At your aunt's house. I remember it well because I stood at the door and watched."

"Don't remind me of it!" Then, more calmly: "No one knew any better then, don't you see? But it's different now. I don't want my son to grow up believing in ghosts and witches."

"He was not scared by a ghost," she said. "After you left I talked to him until he calmed down and made sense in what he said. It was a dog or a coyote that started out of the brush." After a pause she added, "There's nothing wrong in a child being scared of a dog or a coyote, is there?

"He's still a child," she went on. "There's nothing wrong if he's scared by animals."

"What about when he grows up?" Cuitla said. "He'll be scared by animals and say they're spirits."

"Does it matter what it was? Does it matter if it was a spirit or a dog, if the child is scared? Isn't it important at all, what the child feels? And if the healing woman can help him, why should he not go to her?"

He did not answer, and emboldened by her unexpected success she continued, "It is wrong not to believe in anything. It is wrong to mock everything the way you do. How do we know, how do *you* know such things are not true? You laugh, and it is because you have never—"

"Shut up!" he shouted, and she hushed.

He finished taking off his shoes and climbed over her to lie on the other side, by the opening that served as the only window in the hut. He had been forced to lay down the law about that window. She had wanted the bed in the corner, away from the moon, since she was afraid of it, like all the others. They thought the moon did things to people while they slept, and they would have slept in a pigsty if that had been the only place they could crawl into to get away from the moonlight. He wished he could break her of the idea, but he had never been cruel enough to make her sleep on the window side. She could actually get sick, he knew—might even die from it. But he was not afraid to sleep in the light of the moon. Still, it annoyed him to have to climb over his wife every night.

In her own way she was not stupid. She had spoken a great truth a moment ago. Men actually died of fright sickness. If they believed they were going to die. So, though he would not admit it to her, he was satisfied that the boy had gone to the healing woman.

It was cool by the window, almost chilly. He lay there for a long time, thoughts coming and going through his head, memories long forgotten, which with their bustling prevented the emergence of others that lurked in the dark corners of his mind. The Revolution came back to him in one loud dusty mass. Then the sweat and the shouting were gone, and he was back home in his village, sitting in the shade, laughing with some other boys his age while the girls went by to the spring, their earthen jars on their heads, their young hips swinging rhythmically beneath, their bare feet stirring the dust as they went. While the boys watched and laughed. Life had been good.

And now the village was gone and where he was it was hot, but with a different kind of heat, dry and fierce among the white rows. And he felt the tug of the cotton sack behind him and smelled the rancid smell of his own sweat, like old grease in which eggs had been fried. And again he was in the cotton fields of Texas, picking side by side with Jacinto Del Toro, his best friend.

A late moon had risen while he watched the night, and now it floated over the chaparral like a bloated egg yolk. Its rays came in through the window. Cuitla's wife stirred. She edged away from the light, throwing her hair over her face with a nervous movement. She seemed to sleep then, but after a while she stirred again.

"Shall I put up the mosquito net?" she asked.

"What for? There are no mosquitoes."

"It might cut off some of the light. I can't sleep."

"Don't be a damn fool."

"It isn't good," she said. "Not to believe in anything."

He did not answer, so she sighed and turned away. After a while she slept again, but he continued to lie on his back, eyes open, looking at the moon, which now was climbing above the chaparral, white and diminished. It made him sleepy, looking at the moon, and he stopped thinking about the cotton fields of Texas. And the face of Del Toro receded into that of the moon until it finally disappeared and there was nothing but the moon up there. And he kept looking at the moon.

It was a pale, ordinary moon with spots on its face, like the face of a dirty boy, one of those boys that you could see in Texas, boys with skin like half-baked bread. Why were they afraid of it? Tales. They had tales for everything. He floated off for a moment and then rocked back to conscious-ness with a start.

Oh, yes. Tales for everything. Like that rabbit in the moon. The coyote was after it and it jumped, the old people said.

Jumped pretty high, that rabbit.

Américo Paredes

There it was. In the shadow of the moon.

The shadow of the moon. It was very clear. Large. He had never seen it half so large. Never seen the moon so large before. It covered half the sky. An enormous moon. And inside it the shadow grew larger and larger. Larger and darker and darker until it shut out the moon entirely, leaving only a halo visible. Then it started down along the path of the moonrays, slowly at first, then with increasing speed. It came down to earth and slid through the open window with a swoop.

Cuitla woke sitting up in bed, trembling, while his wife held to his arm and called his name.

The first touch of reality was the calling of his name. He was lost, frightened and trembling in the dark, somewhere in awful depths, struggling, mouthing wordless noises. And into the darkness came his name, looking for him, and when his name found him he heard it, waking, heard his wife's voice and he was once again on his bed by the window in the moonlight.

It was some time before he ceased to shake, while his wife held his arm with one hand and stroked the back of his neck with the other. Finally he was calm, and he shrugged her hand away.

"It was a dream," he told her. "Go to sleep."

He lay down on his side, away from her. She did not lie down, but sat looking at him stretched out in the moonlight.

Finally he said, "Well? Are you going to keep watch all night? Go to sleep."

"Don't you think I should call the healing woman?" she asked.

He sat up and peered at her. "Are you crazy?" he said.

"Won't you be reasonable about it? Just because you are a grown man, it doesn't mean that—it doesn't mean . . ."

"Doesn't mean what?"

"That you can't—oh, that man! He almost killed you!"

He slapped her face.

"He almost killed me, that's it? And he scared me, did he?"

"I did not mean it that way," she began, sobs choking her. "I did not mean to say—"

"You did not mean, you did not mean," he said savagely. He slapped her again. "Don't mean anything!"

She buried her face on the pallet and cried while he looked down at her with a mixture of resentment and disgust. Disgust with himself. Wife beating went with brutish ignorance. He was sorry for the weeping woman beside him. A good, simple woman who had made him a faithful wife. But to think such a thing! That poor excuse for a man. Frighten him? Better men had not done that. If only she knew what he had really seen. He shook his head. He had seen nothing. There had been nothing on the road. The thing now was for him to go to sleep. But he could not. He lay there beside his wife, listening to her sobs until they dwindled into convulsive sighs. Finally they died out and were replaced by the regular breathing of sleep.

That old witch. He should have got rid of her long ago, but her husband had been one of his men. He had died bravely. It was no easy task to drive out the wife of a man like that. Even if she went around talking to whirlwinds, fighting hurricanes with enchanted knives, foretelling evil, looking at men's wrists to see if they were possessed.

His left thumb strayed over to his wrist, as if to feel his pulse. The thumb explored among the tendons and cartilage.

Américo Paredes

Suddenly his heart gave a cold little jump. Yes! There it was! A crevice there, as if the cartilage had sprung open.

He flung his hand away. Wrists were made that way, with a soft spot in the middle! He crept out of bed and groped in the shelf close to the fireplace, found the bottle, and gulped down a long drink. Then he went back to bed and slept. He dreamed of cotton fields again, though only with part of his mind.

Chapter 9

He was riding again on the road that went around the fields. Across his saddlebow he carried his rifle again, as he had done that day. But hanging to the saddle horn was something else, a feedbag of woven *ixtle*. In the bag were three round bottles of clear glass, containing liquid as clear as the glass itself. He had just come in from the main road, where he had seen the peddler and sold him some corn for mezcal.

The peddler was conveniently on call. Formerly his visits had been furtive, because Cuitla had forbidden drinking within the colony. But it was different now. The peddler kept up appearances and did not come inside the colony. He stayed just outside, on the road. He did good business selling mezcal for corn. Or for anything else of value.

Cuitla took a few drinks every night to sleep. In the mornings he did not feel very well, but that was because even with the mezcal he did not sleep enough. The men were drinking too, even in the afternoons. And at night he could hear their wild, gleeful yells as they rode about, drinking and singing.

He reined in his horse under the shadow of a tree, took out one of the bottles and drank. The fiery spirits filled him with a warm wholeness. They also gave him a moment of reflection, cozy and self-satisfied, but reflection nonetheless.

"If I were a believer," he thought, "I would think God is playing with me."

Antonio, his mother had named him, after Saint Anthony, who had resisted the devil's temptations even when the fiend appeared to him in the shape of a beautiful naked

woman. He remembered how he had shocked his native village with his version of the legend: If the devil appeared to
him in the shape of a beautiful woman, the devil would get
screwed. The story had gone round, causing laughter and
scandal. It was then that the *jefe político* began to make
inquiries about him, and he had to leave the village for the
first time. But it was a good story, his threat to rape the devil.
It was one he loved to tell his men once the Revolution got
under way. And except for Sánchez, perhaps, they all enjoyed
it, even Del Toro.

A shiver overtook him, and he shrugged his shoulders to
throw it off. He must keep them under control. They must
stay on the land. They must not lose everything through a
foolish attempt at revenge. He had told his wife that he had
the chills and fever, and that he would send to Morelos for
some patent medicine.

"It's sleeping by that open window," she said. "You have
caught cold."

He didn't argue, though he knew what she meant. The
medicine didn't do him any good. He had not expected it to
help. Neither had his wife, he knew.

Meanwhile, they whispered behind his back. But they
never said anything to his face. They were afraid of his rifle,
which he carried on his pommel always. But he went about
with some fear himself, of a bullet from behind a bush some
day.

But they didn't know. If they only knew! A thing of that
sort did not make a man a coward in their eyes. Everything
would be all right then. The healing woman would come, and
he would sleep afterwards without nightmares or fever, without the bottle of mezcal. But then it would all be true. He
could no longer speak against it, could never deny it. No. He
would never sink that low. Sitting around a fire, telling silly

stories. Passing on to others the same ignorance and fear.
He was above that.

He took another drink and put the bottle away. Once you
died, you died, you were gone forever. He picked up the reins.
As he had done now for some time, when he got into one of
these moods, he imagined himself in conversation with Don
José María Jiménez, who now lived in Morelos and came to
visit his lands only rarely. Don José María no longer visited
Cuitla's colony, but that was understandable. They suspected
Don José María, though there was no evidence he had been
involved. Cuitla had pointed that out to the investigator who
had been sent from Morelos. But the men suspected all
landowners.

Don José María had been Cuitla's friend. He could see
the man's smile, and again they were sitting, in chairs, under
the bamboo shade outside Cuitla's hut.

"Life is a dream," Don José María said, as he often did.
He was always thinking up things like that. "And dreams are
also dreams."

Cuitla nodded. "Did I tell you about my dream?" he said.
"Perhaps you can read it for me. But if it is a dream, then yes,
I have dreamed. But please tell me my fortune."

Don José María smiled. "You Indians are all alike," he
said.

Cuitla took out his knife and cut off Don José María's
head, and after that he began to weep.

Then Don José María was whole again. "Of course I did
not mean you," he said. "You wear shoes."

He came fully awake with a start. Perhaps he should stop
somewhere and lie down. Once he had shown Don José

María some poems he had made, and Don José María had taken them away and copied them. He had never told any of the men. Once he had said to him, "How is it that men are born like that? You born here, I so far away. I in a village, you here by the river banks. But yet I feel toward you like a brother." Don José María had smiled his strange smile, so that Cuitla did not know whether he agreed or was laughing at him.

The horse shook its head, and he slackened the reins. Then he jerked them back, so hard the horse nearly sat down on the road.

"No!" he shouted. A shadow fell across the road. "No!" he cried again, as his horse pirouetted while he tried to control it, tried to lift his rifle, and all the while another part of himself tried to keep him from doing all these things.

The horse came down on all four legs. And there in the middle of the road stood old Juan Sánchez, watching him steadily from under his bumpy eyelids. He just stood there, saying nothing, watching him with a sort of crafty deference, his hat in both hands, his figure slightly stooped in a half-bow. Sánchez had never got rid of his peon manners. He had already been old, and must have got along well enough with his master, when the Revolution came and he opened the gates one night so the Zapatistas could cut his master's throat.

Finally Cuitla said, "Well?"

Sánchez hunched his shoulders just a little more. "It's a spirited horse," he said, his face full of cautious interest. "He does not respond easily to the bit."

"True," Cuitla replied. "He almost threw me." The old man just looked at him.

"Put on your hat," Cuitla added. "You're going to get sunstroke."

"Oh, the sun does not bother me." Sánchez put on his hat. "It has burned me through and through already."

There was a short silence. Cuitla sat on his restive horse while Sánchez stood in the middle of the road looking at the horse's dancing legs.

Finally Sánchez said, "A fine horse, a very fine horse."

Cuitla grunted.

"Just like the one you had during the Revolution," Sánchez continued. "One would say it was his brother."

Cuitla scowled.

"I remember it like it was yesterday," Sánchez went on. "In the charge before Torreón, remember? You were out in front on that other horse and even Del Toro was hanging back. And you turned round in your saddle and yelled at us, 'Come on, you bastards! What do you want to die of, child-birth?'"

Cuitla was silent.

"Those were great days, *jefe*," Sánchez added. "You were the bravest man in the whole Division of the North." He sighed. "Ah, those days will not return!"

Cuitla said, "So what are you doing here? Remembering old times or sunning yourself?"

"I was looking for signs."

"Signs?"

"I have had it on my mind. There must have been a horse. The city man could not have walked all the way up here."

"Nobody found a horse."

"There could have been two of them. Riding on one horse."

"Could be."

"It hasn't rained. So I thought I might find some signs."

"Did you?"

"There were signs of a horse on the other side of the road. Droppings."

"And people's tracks?"

"No. I should have looked sooner."

"There is no way of knowing who else was on the horse. If there were two men."

"There must have been. But Del Toro was dead when we got to him. He could not tell us."

"He didn't tell me, either."

"Tell you? When?"

"Just before I killed the city man. Del Toro was here on the road. Right where you are standing now."

Sánchez did not jump away from the spot, as Cuitla had expected. He moved a couple of steps sideways and crossed himself. "I thought something like that might have happened," he said. "You are a brave man. A *catrín* with a gun would not scare you."

"Thanks," Cuitla said.

"But you must do something about it. A thing like that can kill you."

"The healing woman," Cuitla said.

Sánchez nodded.

"I will think about that, but meanwhile I want to talk about it. To you. I haven't told anyone about it, not even my wife. But you are a man with experience. I know I can trust you."

Sánchez nodded.

Cuitla said, "Let's go over there." He pointed to a large mesquite up the road. "We can talk in the shade."

He rode past the tree and dismounted. As he looped the reins on an overhanging branch, Sánchez reached the mesquite. The old man sat down with his back against the trunk, took off his hat and wiped his forehead. Cuitla turned from the horse, his rifle in one hand and the nosebag in the other. He stood watching Sánchez sitting some ten paces away. Then he walked slowly up to the tree.

"Juan."

Sánchez looked up at him. "Yes, *jefe.*"

Cuitla stepped up beside Sánchez and leaned his rifle against the tree. He reached into the nosebag and took out a bottle. "I have much to tell you, Juan, but first we must have a few drinks. It makes talking easier. Here!"

Sánchez took the bottle and drank. Cuitla drank. Then Sánchez drank again. Cuitla sat down beneath the tree and put his rifle across his knees.

"Where's your horse?" he asked.

"In the thicket over there."

"Still riding the stallion?"

Sánchez nodded and smiled.

"He'll kill you some day," Cuitla said.

"I'm not that old yet," Sánchez replied. He offered the bottle.

Cuitla pushed his hand away. "You drink," he said.

Sánchez drank.

"We have been together for a long time," Cuitla said.

Sánchez nodded. "We have," he agreed.

"I can talk openly to you."

Sánchez nodded once again. "You can," he said and took another drink. He offered the bottle.

"You drink," Cuitla said. Sánchez looked at him. Then he drank. "Yes, we've been through a lot together," Cuitla said. "We're old friends, and there should be no secrets between friends. I have a lot to tell you."

Sánchez nodded, a vague look on his face.

"I will tell you why," Cuitla said. "To keep them on the land. Until the land bears fruit."

Américo Paredes

The mezcal had relaxed Juan Sánchez's features. "The land will not bear," he said, slurring his speech a little. "Not until it is cleansed. Blood has been spilled; the land is cursed. You know that."

"It is the men who are cursed. But let us not go into that. Have a drink."

The old man smiled. He raised the bottle to his mouth and took a sip.

"No," Cuitla said. "Not like that. Drink it all."

Sánchez screwed up his eyes. He looked down at Cuitla's rifle, which was pointing at him.

"The whole bottle," Cuitla said. "We have to celebrate."

Sánchez looked thoughtful. Then he drank. When he had drained the bottle, Cuitla reached behind him with his left hand. He took another bottle and tossed it into Sánchez's lap.

"Let's drink this one too," he said.

It was sunset when Antonio returned to the village. He came alone and his *ixtle* nosebag was empty. In the lane between the huts that served as a village street, he encountered the healing woman, led by a child, a dirty little girl dressed in a shift that once had been white. The old woman, in black as always, held the girl by the arm with one leathery claw and tottered beside her, bent and gnarled like an old piece of mesquite, her sightless eyes staring in front of her, her face set in the thoughtful, faraway expression of the blind. She stopped at the sound of horse's hoofs and muttered something to the child.

Then she turned, seeking him with her blank eyes, her stick upraised. "Demon!" she shrieked. "Foul! Foul! Foul!"

Cuitla started back in his saddle. It was an unpleasant surprise, to be taken for another. He forced a smile and answered in an almost jovial tone, "You are mistaken, old woman. I am Antonio Cuitla."

But the old woman kept screaming, "I see you! Fiend! I know you! Demon!"

Heads appeared in neighboring huts, a few children came out into the open and stared. He resisted an impulse to raise his quirt and lay it across her face. Instead he laughed, the way Del Toro had always laughed whenever the old woman had accosted him, and he reined his horse aside, riding away towards his own hut while the old woman screamed until she was led away.

He was glad he had restrained himself, because tomorrow he must talk to her son, Serapio Rendón. Whatever his mother might be, Serapio was the man that Cuitla would need tomorrow. And for a long time after that.

Chapter 10

He had thought it would help, but it had not helped at all. It was like talking to a man already dead. How he had wished during the past weeks that he could have talked to Don José María. With him he could have brought the thing out into the light of day, so it would have ceased to be anything at all. He had thought of going to Morelos, just to see him and talk about it. Once he even put some clothes into a *morral* and got ready to go. But at the last moment he felt too tired to make the trip.

So he had told Juan Sánchez instead, before he put him on the stallion and wound the *reata* round his leg. But Sánchez had been too drunk by then—or perhaps he had known all along, and what Cuitla told him came as no surprise. That sly old man. Not even death had surprised Sánchez in the least. Perhaps he had not heard at all, drunk as he was, and again Cuitla had been talking to himself even before the stallion threw Sánchez off and trampled him to death.

After they picked up the tattered remnants of Juan Sánchez, Cuitla made Serapio Rendón, the healing woman's son, his second-in-command. The men stayed in the fields. With his last strength Cuitla kept them there, working the land, while he rode up and down with the rifle on his saddle bow, until he got too tired to ride every day and began to go out every other day, and finally did not ride out any more. But the men stayed in the fields even then.

Américo Paredes

The days got hotter, and at last the long rows of cotton were topped with white, and the corn grew hard in the ear. But the men did not harvest yet. Serapio Rendón pleaded with them.

They would say, "Oh, tomorrow. Yes, tomorrow. Have a drink, Serapio. You're too young for that sort of thing, Serapio. Here, have a drink. Did you know the cotton buyer is selling beer now? Keeps it in a box with ice. Have a drink."

Serapio would end by drinking with them, lying among them in the shade of the trees that bordered the fields. They lay there panting from the heat of the sun outside and the fire of the mezcal within. And the cotton hung down in streamers. The weevils, the birds, and the field mice ate the corn.

Serapio Rendón would tell them, "Boys, we must get that crop out of the fields. Especially the corn, for corn is life. We plowed it, we cultivated it. Our children watched over it so it could grow. It must be harvested."

The men would grin. "Our children," they would say, nudging each other. "Did you hear that? Our children."

And Serapio would redden, because he was a young man and had no wife.

"Where did you hear all that, Serapio?" they would say. "Who taught you all those words?"

They laughed, waking up those who were napping under the trees, their hats over their faces, to tell them the joke.

Serapio would get angry. "Laugh if you like. But we must get the crop out of the fields, you fools."

"Sure," they said. "Sure, Serapio, don't get mad now, it would hurt our feelings."

"We're going to do it. Tomorrow we'll begin."

The cotton buyer still gave them credit. He was handy to the colony, a ways down the road in a shack he had set up on the Jiménez land. He had bought no cotton yet, but he sold staples, bright things, and drink, on credit. On the crops. He was a pleasant man, a good-hearted man who could refuse no one, least of all the men of Los Claveles. And when they did not feel like going all the way down the road, the peddler still came around, and he was giving credit too.

So they went out to drink in the fields, as far away from Antonio Cuitla as they could. Toward evening they would return to the huts. The more conscientious picked a few ears from the standing corn and carried them home in gunny sacks. As they straggled back from their day in the fields, they gave vent to their high spirits in horseplay and cackling cries. In the village they fell silent. And they avoided passing by the window of Antonio Cuitla's hut.

One gloomy afternoon Cuitla sat on his bed by the window and watched them come back from the fields. They should harvest soon, before it rained and everything went back into the earth again. He should speak to Serapio about it, but the thought made him feel weak and listless. They were coming down the road and into the village. Some of them were carrying their little sacks of stunted ears. It would never occur to them to load some of the mules. That would have been easier and quicker, but their minds did not go that far. They had no wagons. They could have bought some with this year's crop. But there would be no crop.

Once Cuitla had dreamed of a tractor, had seen himself enthroned upon it, driving it up and down the fields. But the tractor, like everything else, had been a dream. As for Del Toro, they had forgotten about him now. No one remembered Jacinto Del Toro except Antonio Cuitla, his old friend.

Américo Paredes

As he sat there thinking about Del Toro and Don José María and the crop rotting in the fields like an unburied corpse, he suddenly felt a surge of strength and decided to call Serapio in for a talk. He sent his boy to catch up with Serapio, and from the window he saw the man stop, undecided, looking toward the hut and away as if he were trying to make up his mind not to come. Finally he nodded and went into his own hut with the gunny sack.

Cuitla sat looking out, waiting for Serapio to come. He preferred to sit that way. Because when he looked out, into the light of day, he couldn't see *it*. But if he looked inside, he saw *it*, sitting in a corner, a shapeless black lump in a corner of the room. But he knew that, though it was there whenever he looked, it really wasn't there at all. He knew it because his mind told him so, his logical reasoning mind. He could logically determine that it was not there at all.

When he had been stronger, he had proved it to himself by experiment. He would rise from his bed, his flesh crawling with fear but driven ahead by a core of hate and pride. He would lunge into the corner where it sat. Triumphant, proud, hating it and hating himself for requiring this proof that it was not there.

But, once more in bed, he could see it again in the corner. It did nothing, it said nothing. It was just there. Sitting, watching. It watched him day and night, though it had no eyes.

Serapio came out of his hut and walked slowly toward Cuitla's. He was a straight, well-fleshed boy, with a round face and tawny eyes. His father had been fair, a transient from the north who had taken up with Anastacia Rendón, the village healer. The woman had bewitched him, people said. Gave him a cup and a half and kept the jar on the coals, as the saying went. But that was all talk.

Cuitla put his hands under the covers before he remembered that his wife had taken it away and put it on the shelf. And he really had no use for it, at least not now. But the sight of Serapio had made him search for it without thinking at all. Serapio came up warily. He approached the window close enough, but not too close, staying just out of reach. Near enough for Cuitla to look into his yellow eyes. He realized that what he did not like about Serapio was his eyes. They looked just like a cat's.

"Come closer, boy," he said. "I want to have a good look at you. It's so long since you last came."

"It's nice to see you," Serapio said. "You are looking well." But he came no closer.

"Thank you," Cuitla said. "I am glad you are concerned about my health."

Serapio did not answer. He just stood there with one foot drawn back, as if ready to duck or run around the corner of the hut.

"Why have you avoided me?" Cuitla asked.

"I have not avoided you," Serapio said. "If I have not come often it is because I have feared to bother you."

Cuitla grinned, feeling his slack skin wrinkle on his face. "You are considerate," he said. Serapio did not reply. "Boy," Cuitla said, "I have loved you like a son."

"Thank you. I am grateful."

"I expected much of you."

"I have tried to obey your orders."

"Oh, you don't have to defend yourself. You don't have to obey. Why obey? We are all disobedient, aren't we? All bad children, disobedient sons accursed and doomed to die."

Serapio took a step back.

"Don't be alarmed," Cuitla said. "It's just a manner of speaking. I was using the words of the *corrido*. Isn't that the way it goes, the one you've been singing in the fields?"

"I don't sing," Serapio said.

"Are you afraid of curses?" Cuitla was amused. "Don't you know we are all accursed? Hasn't your mother told you that?"

"My mother tells me nothing of her affairs."

"When she passes my window she has enough to say."

"She is old and blind, she is not well. She has got it into her head that you are not you but someone else."

Cuitla laughed, just a little laugh. But then he was laughing with his belly, his chest, and even with his arms and legs. Until a hand upon his shoulder shook him. Then he stopped. It was his wife. Serapio was gone. She touched his wasted face with light, careful fingers. Then she threw herself down on her knees beside the bed, taking one of his bony hands in hers, kissing it again and again.

"Why? Why don't you let yourself be cured? You would rather die?"

"Don't be foolish," he said.

She rose to her feet. "You talk in your sleep," she said. Then in a whisper, "What does he say? What does he do?"

"Stop it!" he cried, his voice suddenly strong. "I'll hit you in the mouth!"

She did not draw back.

"She's out there again, isn't she? I won't have her in here, I tell you!" He half-raised himself, his voice quavering. "I'll shoot her if she comes in here again."

"Hush, hush," she said, bending over him again. "She isn't there. She is not coming in."

"Where . . . where . . . ?" He felt among the covers for the pistol that was not there.

She gently pushed him down. "You have the fever again," she said.

Chapter 11

He was at the bottom of a sea of fire. Then he shot up like a released cork and came out with a pop that made his ears ring. He shivered and coughed and lay there on the surface. Dark, shiny things glimmered upon it.

The shadow was still there in the corner, and he talked to it as to a houseguest who has lingered too long. "Why don't you go away?" he told it. "Leave off. Forget this hunger of yours."

The shadow just stood there as it had done on the road. It looked like a squat black stone, and from the bed it looked just as solid. "Is it blood you want? You big black monkey cut out of rock. Is it blood you want?"

The steps were black with blood. High above the marketplace. There it sat, there he sat. Black and immovable, while the others gathered round and fell flat on their faces. The healing woman came up in a robe of feathers, a knife in her hand, and she rushed towards Antonio Cuitla crying, "My son! My son!"

He stifled a scream and jolted back to consciousness. The shadow was no longer there. It had gone away, but he knew it would be back.

He shifted his weight in bed and said aloud, "Man is a beast that dreams and nothing more, a beast that dreams."

"He is a rope," Don José María said, "with one end higher than the other, don't you think, *señor presidente?* Yet, is it worth it? One wonders at times. Is it fair, do you think, is it even good? Why teach an ape to read?"

"Perhaps that is a little strong," Cuitla said.

"Oh, don't misunderstand me," Don José María said. "I believe in progress, I am as patriotic as the next man. But is it not so? The priests just varnished them over. And gave them Spanish names. But it still is there, underneath."

It was still there, squatting in the corner where it always was, watching him without eyes. "Man makes himself," he told the shadow. "Everything is possible."

It made no sign.

"Man can rise to the surface," Cuitla said, "with a little pop that makes his ears ring. He has even made for himself a soul. But it is of his own making. There is no Hereafter, there is no God, and you do not exist."

The shadow was still there.

"Oh, why don't you go away. Go away, damn it. Go away!"

His wife came hurrying into the room. "There, there," she said. "It has gone away. It has gone away."

She gave him something to drink, and he found the pride to murmur, "What has gone away? What are you talking about?"

He lay back, exhausted, and the fever swallowed him again. He was burning inside. He was thirsty, so thirsty that he knew he would die if he did not drink something clear and cold. If he could just have a jar full of water, he did not care what happened afterward. But he would not ask for it.

And there he was again, standing in the middle of the room as he had done before, his mouth like a dry, blind fire. And there it was on the table right in front of him, in a large earthen jar that had been smoothly shaped and then fired and glazed so that the glaze threw back a cool reflection of the light. A jar made of brown clay that gave the water its own clay flavor, its own tangy rainwater taste. Brimming with cool, clear water that made little ripples just below the rounded lip, while tiny drops beaded the clay outside like sweat.

He took a joyful step toward it and stopped. They would not fool him again. He wasn't going to take it. They couldn't make him, however they tried. He stopped, his hands outstretched. But his mouth burned, and he knew they would have their way unless he did something to prevent it. He would knock it off the table. He put out his hand.

Then he had it in both hands, seized tightly, squeezed between his fingers. He had it now! He raised it to his lips. He could see the clearness and the coolness of it.

And then they were all laughing at him. A spluttering laughter, as if they were trying to control it at first and could not. And then peals of it, as they lost all pretense, all respect. They laughed at him while the thing in his hands squirmed. It was a doll that looked like the healing woman, twisting this way and that in his hands and trying to get away. Then it stopped and raised a tiny arm and pointed at his face. "Evil! Evil!" it said.

This brought another roar of laughter from the crowd. They were all around him, holding their sides and laughing, their mouths open wide in their big dark faces. They laughed and laughed, and then the faces began to grow, while their bodies disappeared and he was surrounded by huge Indian faces, all laughing at him.

He yelled at them with the deep authoritative voice of old times, and they ran. But they looked back as they went and laughed. He doubled up his fists and ran after them, to strike at them, to smash the great noses and make the big mouths run with blood. But as they ran from him they would stoop and pick up pieces of the land, great big pieces which left enormous holes yawning into emptiness, so he had to stop and then run around the holes. And he could never catch up with them.

"Come back!" he shouted at them. "What do you want to die of? Childbirth?"

But they ran all the harder, stooping and laughing as they ran, going in broad circles just to taunt him and to make him lose his breath. And he saw they were moving down a road, and that at the far end of the road was one who did not run, but stood spraddle-legged in the middle of it. And Antonio Cuitla followed them toward this one who did not run but who suddenly began to grow as Cuitla approached. And when he got near he looked up and saw it was Del Toro, huge and black against the sky. And he looked as he had looked the last time. Even the wounds were showing. And they bled just a little as he stood there, enormous against the sky. With his eyes closed and not laughing like the others, but with a quiet smile upon his face as if he knew something he did not want to tell.

When Cuitla saw Del Toro he gave a scream of rage and threw the doll to the ground. And it was a jar, which broke into pieces, and the water splashed out in a cool shower on the earth, drenching Cuitla's feet. He fell on his face, his burning mouth open, but before he could drink it the water sank swiftly into the earth. It sank without a trace, and he lay there on his face, eating the dust, digging into the hard earth with his teeth. And above him he could hear their laughter.

He could hear them laughing as he slowly rose. Still feverish, he sat up in bed, the sound of laughter outside like water falling. He pushed out of bed and sat on the edge of it, his feet resting on the bare, alkali dirt, forgetting to step onto his shoes, as was his custom. It was dusk. A fire had been lighted in the plaza-like space in front of his hut. The flames

shone through the window, lighting up the corners of his hut
with a moving pattern of lights and shadows. The men were
gathered around the fire outside. He could hear them laughing about something. Some joke, perhaps.

Someone was passing his fingers over the strings of a
guitar, caressing them, pressing a thumb over them as one
does with an ear of ripe corn, so that the notes pattered
down like grain. Cuitla rose shakily from his bed. Outside the
guitar began to pour out a succession of smooth notes that
slipped down and were lost in the night, like drops of water
falling. The guitar spoke its invitation to the voices, and the
voices answered. They sang of the disobedient son. The
same song they had been singing yesterday, and many other
yesterdays, a song brought up north from the hot lands
where they had been born.

Cuitla held on to the bed. When the chill passed, he
groped his way forward, seeking the way out.

Sword in hand, the son threatened his father, and the
father cursed the son. Humbly he lay, waiting for death.

Cuitla staggered toward the table, the notes of the guitar
falling on his fever.

Let the son be buried in the wild and lonely earth. His
arm will stick out of his grave, and in his hand there shall be
a paper with gilded edges, on which shall be written that his
was a life accursed.

On the shelf was the beautiful foreign automatic that had
been the stranger's. He reached up and coaxed it from the
shelf with the tips of his fingers. Finally it came down to him,
so suddenly that it almost slipped from his grasp. It was
smooth and heavy and felt good to the touch. He rubbed it
between his hands.

The bull came down from the mountain. They had never
brought him down, but now he came, with the herd all about
him. The black bull that had never left the hills.

And now he was standing at the door. They were seated in a half-circle about the fire, their faces transformed, their mouths half open, their eyes shining in the light. Before them the singers sang, with their eyes shut and their heads thrown back, with an intense application to their task, as though they sang not from enjoyment but from a compelling need. Cuitla stood leaning against the doorway, watching them. He hated them because he knew that to them he was already dead. He . . .

It was only a horse which somebody had left hitched to a post beside his house. Somebody who had been in a hurry to get to the gathering by the fire and had left the horse there, saddled and bridled by the post. He poked the gun into his belt and staggered toward the horse, supporting himself along the wall of the hut until he got to it and put his hands on the cool smooth leather of the saddle. There was a clean smell about the leather, a cleanness identified with the sweat of the horse and the smell of its urine mixed with earth. A wholeness that he had almost forgotten about, lying there on his bed.

He struggled into the saddle and took the reins, while the singers sang about the bull, the black bull of the mountain in the light of the eastern star.

He burst upon them out of the dark, flogging the horse into a gallop and riding straight into the flames. The horse reared as it hit the fire, scattering burning fagots all about. The men scattered too. They ran to the edge of the clearing and stood there for a moment. Then they saw the gun in his hand, and they scattered into the dark. He checked the frightened animal and walked it round and round the flames, shaking the pistol at the dark, for he could see no one, though he knew that they were there.

"Come out!" he cried. "I order you!" He fired his pistol into the air. No one moved into the light.

"I am Antonio Cuitla!" he yelled hoarsely. "I am Antonio Cuitla, father of all you bad boys! Don't kneel before me, I am not the bishop! I whip little boys when they don't behave! I eat brave men and shit on cowards! Ah-hah-hah-eee!"

No one took up the challenge. "Is there anybody out there?" he shouted, his voice breaking. "Are there any men there? Any men left at all? Who is there in the dark, listening, listening?"

He brought the horse to the edge of the dark, peering. "I see you!" he shouted suddenly. "Don't hide behind them!" He fired another shot into the air.

The families living in the huts close by had been slipping into the chaparral. He sensed their blurred movement in the dark and fired into it. A woman screamed in pain, fear, and outrage. Others began howling in sympathy. Children wailed, and there was a quick rush of feet away from Cuitla. He heard the trample and, thinking they were coming toward him, he raised himself in his stirrups, as he had done in battle just before a charge.

"Come in to where it's nice!" he yelled. "Come get your loaves hot from the oven!"

They fled deeper into the chaparral. He was left alone in the village, riding round and round the dying fire, still challenging the dark.

They could hear his spent shouts. Some of them climbed trees, and from there they watched him riding round and round the circle of light. They saw him pull crazily at the reins, saw the horse rise on its hind legs, seeking the ground desperately with its forefeet, fighting the bit and slipping in the soft dirt. They saw him point the pistol, as if to fire, and heard him shout something they did not understand. Then the horse fell to the ground, its frightened squeal drowning him out.

Chapter 12

They came back after they saw him fall. In twos and threes they approached him as he lay on the ground beside the horse, almost in the fire. Cautiously, with catlike little steps, as if expecting him to rise again with a furious shout. But he just lay there, breathing in short rasping breaths. Then the horse rose to its feet and bolted with a rush of air and leather straight through them, and they bolted too. They ran back out of the circle of fire.

Once in the dark, they stopped and laughed at themselves in nervous little chuckles. And they came to him again. This time they gathered round and stood looking down at him as he lay in the dust. Those who had been holding his wife now let her go, and she came running forward. As she ran, her breathing became a sob, and when she reached the group of men it became a scream. The men shrank aside to let her pass. Screaming, she threw herself upon her husband. The other women took up the wail from where they stood in the dark, and now they came forward too.

When they saw he was not dead, the other women stopped their wailing. Only his wife kept up her screaming. It took two men to tear her away from her husband so others could pick him up and carry him into his hut. They laid him on his bed, while others pressed into the hut, some of them carrying fagots from the fire to light their way. A woman started a fire in the fireplace.

His wife stopped screaming suddenly. "Not there," she said. "Not there."

"Not where?" one of the men asked. "Not on his bed?"

"Move it away from the window. Get it as far from the window as you can."

The man looked at her, then nodded. They moved the bed into the far corner of the hut.

On his bed of sticks Cuitla stopped his hoarse breathing and began to curse. He flailed about so much that it took several men to hold him down. At times he broke their grip and sat up before they were able to force him down again. He would weaken then, while they gasped for breath and looked at one another. Then he would try again to break free, and they had to struggle with him again, until the bed broke and they all crashed to the ground.

There was little left of the bed but splinters, so what remained of it was taken outside. The pallet was laid on the ground. It was easier to hold him down this way. Only two men were needed to guard him. Others could take turns so there would always be two men, one at his head and one at his feet, to bear down on him and pin him to the earth when a fit of fury assailed him. The rest gathered about in the hut, and it became stifling hot inside. Cuitla's wife and Serapio Rendón were standing by the fireplace. She had stopped crying now and looked on Serapio with fierce determination.

"This is not a natural sickness," she said.

Serapio looked at her intently, his round face shimmering and vague in the light of the fireplace.

"It is not what you think," she said in a querulous voice. "It is not what all of you have thought."

"I don't know," Serapio said. "I don't know what to think."

"I saw it," the woman said. "It was no natural sickness. I saw it with my own eyes."

"You saw it?"

"By God's life I saw it. Once, only once. It was sitting on his chest."

"You didn't do anything?"

"He wouldn't let me. He threatened to kill me."

"It was *it*," Serapio said, a shudder in his voice. "It wouldn't let him." He started quickly toward the door.

"You wronged him," Cuitla's wife called after him. "You wronged my husband."

But he was gone, running between the huts to look for his mother. Cuitla's wife turned to the people in the hut. "You wronged him, all of you," she said loudly. "All of you, you have wronged my husband."

Some of them bowed their heads and went out of the hut. The others stared at Antonio Cuitla and then out into the dark. A whisper began among them, almost like a sigh. It became a rustle and presently it was a hum that grew louder and louder and turned into an uproar as everyone tried to talk at once.

Suddenly the talking ceased. The healing woman was at the door. A step behind her was Serapio, who had guided her there but whose hand she had shaken off as soon as she touched the door. The sick man's ravings sank to a mumble in the sudden quiet, while she stood at the doorway survey-ing the scene with her sightless eyes. Her face was deeply scarred by the smallpox that had eaten out her eyes.

A canvas pouch hung by a string from the rope belt around her waist. There was a crude rosary about her neck, into which empty spools of thread were strung, intermingled with glass beads and pieces of coral. She leaned on her stick, moving her head now to one side, now to the other, as if she were looking over the room. But on her face was a distant, inward-looking air. Then she seemed to come to life again, back from wherever she had been behind the darkness of her eyes.

She raised her head. "Out with you!" she cried shrilly. "Out with all of you! Out!"

At the sound of her voice Cuitla began to struggle again, echoing her words: "Out! Out!"

"You see," Serapio told his mother. "Someone has to stay."

"You, then," she said. "You and another."

She groped her way to the fire and, reaching into her pouch, she threw a handful of herbs on the flames. A sickly sweet smoke filled the room and the crowd scurried out. At the door Serapio put his hand on Lupe Melguizo's arm and held him back.

"You stay with me," he said.

Lupe Melguizo's Adam's apple bobbed up and down in his long neck. He nodded, not trusting himself to speak, and went reluctantly to Cuitla's pallet. The two took over the job of holding the sick man down. The men they relieved quickly left the hut. Now the healing woman threw a handful of something else on the fire, and the sweetish smell became foul. The smoke rolled out in billows. Lupe coughed and let go of Cuitla with one hand to cross himself.

Outside, the whole colony was gathered. Mothers suckled their babies, craning their necks and saying "Hush! Hush!" when the baby let go of the breast and seemed about to cry. Close to the door in a semicircle were six men, all past middle age, who stood facing the hut as if waiting for a signal from inside. The man on one end had in his hands a black shawl, very narrow and long. He kept crumpling and smoothing it out. It was he who stood so he could look into the hut.

"She has the ashes now," the man said, without turning toward the others. A low murmur passed through the crowd, a kind of fearful assent.

"Now she has made the crosses," the man said. "The ashes are still hot." The crowd murmured again.

"She is sweeping him now."

Inside, Cuitla struggled to escape the men who held him down.

The little girl who led the healing woman about now made her appearance, a piece of cloth clutched tightly in her hand. The men moved aside to let her inside, and the crowd began to murmur again.

"It's a piece of his shirt."

"No, from his underdrawers."

"Lucky that Felipa had not washed them."

The little girl came out again, and the man on the end of the semicircle waved his hand behind his back at the crowd. The murmurs died out behind him, and the silence crept back until even those farthest from the entrance were still.

"Now she's smoking him," the man said looking into the hut.

Suddenly the man tensed and said loudly, "Now!"

He quickly unrolled the shawl and passed the length of it to the other five, holding on to his end, until the six held the shawl fully stretched, tightly in their hands. A deeper hush fell upon the crowd. From inside the hut came the healing woman's voice, raised in a series of half-intelligible words, then a drone that sounded like a prayer.

She stopped abruptly and cried out in an urgent voice, "Come! Come to me! Come!"

Quickly the man on the end of the shawl tied a knot into it, tightened the knot hastily and gripped it in both hands. The healing woman resumed her muttering, drowned out now and then by Cuitla's screams.

Then again came her urgent voice, "Come! Do not leave me! Come!" Another knot was tied.

The first man turned to his neighbor. "It moves!" he whispered. "It moves!" The knot in his hands shook.

Américo Paredes

They looked about them with anxious eyes, searching for some animal that would leave the hut, some black formless shape, creeping or flying.

A third knot was tied. But still, nothing came. The healing woman's voice droned on and on. Then she cried out in a high wail resembling Cuitla's scream that followed it as response, "Come! Come!"

The fourth knot was tied.

A humming noise had been hanging in the air behind the crowd, faint at first, almost like a murmur. Now it grew until it became a drone. Then it was no longer a drone but a coughing roar, and a broom of light moved across the dark and swept away the blackness before Antonio Cuitla's hut. The shaft of light roved about until it settled on the entrance.

Automobiles had arrived on the main road, and their headlights had been turned upon the crowd. The healing woman's voice stopped. The hands on the shawl relaxed. The crowd broke into one excited babble and then subsided into complete silence as the motors were turned off. The sick man's raving also stopped, and in the brilliantly lighted silence only his noisy breathing could be heard.

Chapter 13

Brigadier Miguel Angel de la Portilla was annoyed, with a manifold annoyance that worked deep into his skin. He was annoyed at his corporal-chauffeur for having allowed the car to break down. He was annoyed at himself for having struck the corporal in the face, something that should no longer happen in the army of a democratic society, though the corporal did not know he belonged to a democratic army.

But the brigadier's annoyance went deeper than that. He was annoyed at the dust, at the heat, at the city of Morelos, in which he must waste precious years of his life as commandant. He was annoyed at his old friend, the lawyer from the capital, who sat beside him in the sedan, who had insisted on coming along and had seen him hit the corporal. Annoyed even more that a prominent citizen of Morelos should also be in the sedan. Still another witness to the general's lack of self-control. And now Brigadier Miguel Angel de la Portilla was annoyed at what he saw.

The brigadier was new in the municipality of Morelos. He was making his first tour of the agrarian colonies. Someone in Mexico City had decided that this should be one of his duties, to check on the progress of the Revolution and report his findings, with the required number of carbons, to the national capital. It was not a duty in which he found pleasure, though Brigadier de la Portilla was a conscientious man.

He was perhaps a bit too proud of his education and of the lightness of his skin, but he had been a liberator, though a tardy one. He firmly believed in the Revolution. He was a man of principle, in spite of what his friend the lawyer thought. He loved these people, for whom he had sacrificed his fortune and risked his life. Though it was true—as the lawyer loved to slyly remind him—he would have lost his fortune and put his life in peril in any case. But he loved his people, though they did manage to annoy him more than they should at times. And this was one of those times.

The brigadier leaned out of the car, took a good look at the scene before him and cursed. He swore with the roundness and verve of a Spaniard, though he had never been in Spain.

"¡Hi de puta, putos!" he said. Then he added, as an afterthought, "¡Hijos de la Gran Putaña!"

Thus having consigned the whole colony to whoredom, he rapped on the side of the car with his riding crop so someone would come and open the door.

"What *is* the matter?" asked his friend the lawyer, his voice tinged with bored curiosity. "Just what is happening, anyway?" He was a spare, thin-lipped man in a double-breasted suit and a soft felt hat that made him look more like a detective than a lawyer.

"As if you didn't know," the brigadier replied.

"Why no," the lawyer said. "I don't." He turned to the man on his left. "Perhaps you can enlighten me, Don José María."

"It's one of their rituals," the brigadier interrupted scornfully. "One of their savage rites. You see now what we're up against. What can you do with people like that? Except stand them up against a wall and shoot them. Eh?"

"Effective suffrage, no reëlection," the lawyer said. "All men are created equal." He was a cynical man.

"Bah!" the brigadier said, as the corporal with the swollen lip came and opened the door for him.

He alighted, his step springy, his little form erect, twisting at his mustache, slapping his leg with the riding crop, while a lieutenant and a squad of soldiers piled out of the truck behind and formed in front of the gate. The corporal opened the gate and the squad presented arms as the brigadier marched in, then followed close behind him.

"What's this?" the brigadier said brusquely, addressing all of them and no one in particular. "What sort of gathering is this?"

They all gaped at him, and he went into the hut before anyone could answer, if any had dared to. A soldier with a lantern followed him, and the headlights were turned off.

The inside of Cuitla's hut became dark again, except for the diluted light shed by the lantern. The brigadier looked about him with his terrible little eyes and saw the healing woman. She had tried to shrink into a corner, blending into the shadows. But the light of the lantern found her out.

"You!" the brigadier said. "What are you doing in here?"

She just looked toward him with her blind eyes.

"Get out," the brigadier said. Then he amended his order. "Get her out."

A soldier came forward, took her gingerly by the arm and led her out. When he had handed her over to one of the crowd outside, he came back wiping his palm against his trouser leg, wiping and wiping as if he wanted to give the cloth a high polish. The brigadier pretended not to notice.

"Where is this man's wife?" he demanded.

The soldier beside him looked toward the door and, addressing the crowd, repeated, "Where is his wife?"

Outside another soldier echoed, "His wife?"

The brigadier's demand progressed through the crowd, as though carried on a wave. There was a stir and Cuitla's wife appeared, pushed forward by others. She came to the brigadier with eyes downcast, picking at the front of her skirt.

"What is the matter with your husband?"

"With your permission," she said, "he has been given a sickness."

"Sickness? *Given?*" he demanded, though he knew well what she meant.

"A made-up sickness, your grace. With your permission."

The brigadier snorted. "Nonsense!" he said.

She bowed her head and then moved aside as a sergeant came in. The sergeant stepped forward and saluted.

"If it please my general," he said, "I have something to report."

"Report," the brigadier said listlessly.

"He is the president of the colony," the sergeant said. "He got drunk and shot up the village. Wounded a woman. His horse fell on him just a little while ago." He saluted.

The brigadier laughed a short, unpleasant laugh. "That's it, eh? The bottle, eh?" He laughed again and slapped his leg lightly with his riding crop.

Abruptly he took the lantern from the soldier's hand and approached the pallet where Antonio Cuitla lay. He brought the lantern up to Cuitla's face, and the dying eyes gleamed dully in reflected light. The brigadier looked at the wasted face topped with gray matted hair, the brown seamed face, wrinkled deep around the eyes and mouth. He scowled.

"Brutes!" he said. "Animals!" He gave the lantern back to the soldier and walked out. The lawyer and Don José María had just come into the hut. They stood aside to let him pass.

"You knew the man?" the lawyer asked.

"Quite well. He was my friend."

The lawyer smiled.

"Seriously," the other said. "He was seeking my assistance. That's why I asked to come along with you. I am greatly indebted to you and the general."

"He needs no help," the lawyer said. "Not now."

Don José María turned to the soldier. "Allow me, friend," he said, taking the lantern. He approached the pallet, bringing the light up to Cuitla's face.

"Antonio," he said, "can you hear me? It is I, José María, your friend."

Cuitla stirred, seeking the voice.

"It is I, José María. I got your letter. We have much to talk about."

The lawyer came and stood at Don José María's elbow. "He can't understand you," he said.

Don José María ignored him. "Maybe you've heard the news, Antonio," he said. "About the highway to the sea. A paved road fourteen feet above the ground all the way from Morelos to the gulf. We will take our cotton to the gin in trucks. That will be progress. The *estero* will be drained. Then there will be bottom land for everybody. Much land, Antonio."

The lawyer took the lantern from Don José María and gave it back to the soldier. "Come," he said gently, "let us go out into the fresh air." He took Don José María's arm. "I did not know he had been so good a friend. But it is of no use, he does not understand."

Don José María shook off the lawyer's hand and almost lost his balance. The lawyer took him by the shoulders to keep him from falling.

"He *does* understand!" Don José María said with desperate earnestness. "Didn't you see his eyes?"

"It was the gleam of the lantern. A reflection only."

Américo Paredes

Don José María hung his head for a moment, then replied in a much calmer tone: "I wanted him so much to understand."

"Was he ill for long?"

"A couple of months ago he was healthy and strong. Now look at him."

"Galloping consumption."

"The people around here say it was *susto*."

"Fright sickness? I thought that was a child's disease."

"It occurs in grown persons also, so they say. A spirit catches a person unawares and takes possession of his soul. And destroys it."

"Hmm," said the lawyer. "I might agree that there are things which can destroy men's souls. But I'm putting my money on galloping consumption."

Again he took Don José María's arm. "Come. Let the man die in peace. And let us get out into the fresh air. Holy Christ! It stinks in here!"

Pioneers of Modern U. S. Hispanic Literature
A series celebrating our recent literary heritage

Since its founding by Dr. Nicolás Kanellos in 1979, Arte Público Press has become the largest and most accomplished publisher of contemporary U. S. Hispanic literature. Beginning in 1992, the press also launched the "Recovering the U. S. Hispanic Literary Heritage" series. This project is the first nationally coordinated attempt, by renowned scholars, to recover, index, and publish historically important "lost" Hispanic writings that date back as far as the American colonial era.

However, U. S. Hispanic authors first began breaking into the mainstream in English during the period following World War II. In some cases, though, their ground-breaking books were haphazardly distributed, or received scant critical attention at the time, or for whatever reason soon became hard to find. To revitalize these works and make them widely available to the reading public—in some cases for the first time ever—Arte Público has created the "Pioneers of Modern U. S. Hispanic Literature" series. These landmark works, by seminal Mexican-American, Puerto Rican, and Cuban-American writers, have been chosen for their historical importance, their authentic representation of the cultures they depict, their lasting influence upon U. S. literature, and their excellence as literature. Among the opening authors and books of the series:

Alba Ambert — *Porque hay silencio*

Américo Paredes — *The Shadow*

Louis Pérez — *Coyote*

Virgil Suárez — *The Cutter*

Jose Yglesias — *A Wake in Ybor City*